Demon Daddy

THE FAERIE PRINCE'S HEART

KD ELLIS

ENTWINED PUBLISHING

The Faerie Prince's Heart
ISBN # 978-1-80250-245-9
©Copyright KD Ellis 2025
Cover Art by Kelly Martin ©Copyright June 2025
Interior text design by Entwined Publishing
Published by Enchant, an Entwined Publishing imprint

Published in 2025 by Entwined Publishing, United Kingdom.

Entwined Publishing is a division of Totally Entwined Group Limited.

Entwined Publishing books by KD Ellis

Out in Austin
Teddy's Truth
Shiloh's Secret
Trusting Tennyson
Loving Lennox

Demon Daddy
The Blood Demon's Pet
The Blood Demon's Collar
The Changeling's Faerie Prince
The Faerie Prince's Heart

Collections
Sold to the Billionaire: A Light at the End

THE FAERIE PRINCE'S HEART

Dedication

To my mom, for the many MANY hours you sat with me at McDonald's while I wrote. Love you more than the universe!

Chapter One

Rory

The Dead Woods are exactly as their name suggests — dead. Standing timber, dry as bone. The trees look brittle as ash, their trunks coated in dark soot and exposed roots little more than kindling. The air is thin, my breath coming fast as we leave the desert behind us. Finally, I can't resist, crouching down to run my fingers through the dirt.

It is dry as chalk. Every step we take sends clouds of off-white powder billowing around us. While it irritates my nose and threatens to make me sneeze, it has some benefits. When it settles, drifting slowly down with nary a breeze to bother it, our footsteps are covered. Vanished, as if we had never walked here.

Aries is ahead of me, his steps silent as he leads Zephyr. He is graceful as a deer as he climbs over a fallen tree, so desiccated that it would be impossible to identify the genus, and Zephyr leaps it with ease.

I clamber over behind them. The fallen tree crumbles beneath my knee when my weight lands on it and I yelp as I lose my balance.

"Careful," Aries says as he catches me, his hands on my arms as he helps me to my feet and steadies me. I never feel clumsy until I am around him.

"Was there a fire?" I wonder out loud.

"Perhaps," Aries answers. Zephyr stomps his foot and tosses his head, his loose reins whipping over his neck. He nudges Aries with his muzzle and I swear his golden eyes are watching me with jealousy.

Aries releases me, patting the horse's neck before he continues speaking. "We know little about the Wilds. Few dare to venture here and even fewer return. Those who do… Well, best not to speak of them."

He looks rattled at whatever memories my question has stirred. Goosebumps rise on my flesh, though it is far from cold. I want to press, to search for any hint at what is to come. But perhaps he is right. Maybe it is best if I do not know. So few of the horrors I've witnessed in Faerie have caused him to flinch. Whatever is bothering him now must be truly terrible.

Spiders crawl down my spine. I tamp down the fear.

We walk for ages before I see the first sign of life.

A small green stalk barely the size of my pinky finger with two limp yellow petals drooping from the white pistil at the center. It should feel hopeful. Instead, it looks sad.

We continue walking. Soon enough, the small sprig is not the only growing thing. As the second sun reaches its zenith, I feel like I've stepped through a looking glass and into a lush rainforest. The air is thick, hot and muggy, and I am grateful for the tall trees with their large fronds that give us shade. The ground is soft and squishy. I lose the shredded fabric protecting my feet quickly as it is sucked into the mud and sticks.

Even the smell is intoxicating. I try to think of a comparison, but nothing is quite right. It is sweeter than strawberries, crisper than a fresh cut apple. It sends my stomach rumbling. I've barely pressed my hand to my abdomen to quiet it when I see the fruit tree.

Golden orbs dangle from the tree branches, each one the size of my fist and lightly glowing. I take a step toward them. Then Aries grips my arm tight, stopping me in my tracks.

I bare my teeth as I spin to face him, hunger overriding everything else. My jaws ache, a telltale sign that my mouth is full of daggers. Would I prefer meat? Of course. There is nothing like smoked jackrabbit to fill a belly, but right now the mysterious fruit smells better even than that.

Aries' eyes widen slightly but he doesn't let go, not even in the face of my monster. His skin is cold against mine. "Rory…" he says, voice trailing off as I growl.

"Hungry," my monster speaks with my mouth. I taste copper on my tongue.

"I don't like the look of them," Aries answers. How brave he is, to contradict my beast with his teeth out.

"I don't like the look of you," my monster says, ever a rebellious teenager, but the mulish answer is enough for me to regain control of my mouth. Pulpy silver needles fall to the dirt. I lift my hand to my throbbing face.

Aries looks wary, his hand slow as he extends it toward me. "We should keep moving."

I allow him to lead me away but I can't resist looking over my shoulder. The once-golden orbs are now cloying gray and red, sticky with mucus and lumpy with fat. They spasm weakly in time with my heartbeat.

Each shuddering pulse sends off-white slime leaking down the moist flesh.

They still smell sweet.

I turn my face away.

I do not thank Aries for his intervention, though I know not what he saved me from. I fear I can guess. Here, near the base of a willow weeping salt, I see a cage of bone. Nestled within is an inflorescence of white orchids.

There, by a craggy boulder, is a spray of knucklebones.

* * * *

Dusk falls but we keep walking, until my soles feel shredded and it's a miracle that I'm not leaving bloody footprints behind. I'm determined not to slow us down, and in truth, it is Zephyr who stops us.

As we reach a stream, the water flowing dark and oily, Zephyr rears. He tosses his head, his loud whinny splitting open the night. Aries grabs his reins and I watch, breath bated, as he struggles to restrain him. Foam flies from the horse's maw. I shouldn't notice, the timing is terrible, but I can't help but see how Aries' muscles cord and bulge, his skin glistening.

Then Zephyr lands one of his dinner-plate hooves on Aries chest and sends him flying—right into the oil-slick river. He sinks slowly, as if in quicksand, and I am moving without thought.

On my knees on the bank, I sink my hands, now tipped with claws curving like fishhooks, into the sickeningly thick warm water until they snag on something fabric. I drag him out, coughing and sputtering, barely noticing the large gouges my nails have left in his chest and arms. I am too busy pounding his back as he vomits sludge.

Only once he draws in his first ragged breath do I have time to feel guilty at the blue blood staining his skin. It is enough for me to shed my claws, leaving raw red fingertips in their place.

"Zephyr," Aries says, gaze pained as he stares at the empty stretch of grass where the horse once stood. While I'd been dragging Aries from the river, the horse must have fled. Should I feel bad for not prioritizing the horse? Would Aries, being a faerie, have been able to survive in the dark water while I restrained Zephyr? *Could* I have restrained him, even if I tried?

"If he is anything like Nexus," I say, speaking of his sire, "he will find his way back to safety on his own."

"I hope you are right." Aries' voice breaks. There is more emotion in him now for Zephyr than I've ever heard from him for me. It turns me to stone while breaking me into pieces.

I push myself to my feet and hesitate before I hold my hand out to Aries. He takes it as if nothing is wrong and allows me to pull him to standing.

I want to cry, for myself and the things that could have been if he was a different person, if *I* was a different person. To let my anger strike him for the injustice of his worry for a horse that he's rarely shown for me.

"We should not cross this water in the dark," is all I say instead. My forearms itch where I submerged them, skin writhing as if bugs have crawled beneath it.

Aries stands statue still, but his shadow, cast from the dim moonlight filtering through the canopy above us, sways from side to side. I lift my gaze to Aries' eyes and they are black, pupils blown.

He allows me to lead him farther up the banks, away from the water and toward an uprooted tree. I guide Aries into the exposed cradle knoll. He is compliant — too compliant to be natural. I am suddenly reminded of the Gravel Girls. The synthetic salts had been introduced to treat severe arthritis.

I don't know who first discovered that chewing it gave users a heroin high without the come down, or how desperate they must have been to try it. I will never forget the sight of their paper-thin skin and broken teeth, or their chemical-born haunted happiness.

I can only hope that whatever magic the water holds, it releases Aries quickly. As he sinks into the dirt depression, his antlers catch briefly in the exposed root system. The weedy, tentacle-like vines knot around the spines and fix him in place, a nature made bondage. Old resentment urges me to leave him tangled. It will still be nothing like the suffering I've felt at his hands or by his orders.

I start untying the curling roots anyway. One antler is freed and the second nearly so when Aries moans. I freeze, stilling my fingers as he meets my gaze. Without thinking, I had straddled his waist to reach his surroyal tines. Now I can feel his manhood between my thighs.

I leave him caught in the vines as I scramble off him, heat flooding my face.

"Ruari," Aries moans my old name, his voice broken and breathy. "I need you. Come to me as you once did." His voice sounds lucid but sweat beads along his brow above his glassy eyes.

"Never that," I murmur. If I allow him to take me again, to claim my body fully with his, it will only ever be like it was. We will come together as equals or nothing. "Sleep, Aries. You are not yourself."

"I am more myself than I have ever been," Aries argues. His hands, not bound by anything, lower to the closure of his trousers. I suck in a breath to tell him to stop but he is too quick for me. That, or maybe I don't want it badly enough.

His erection is engorged and leaking.

Is it the effects of the water? I was immersed up to my shoulders and all I feel is itchy. But I was careful not to swallow the greasy slick, and he drank enough to drown a horse.

"Come to me, Ruari," Aries repeats his plea, his slender fingers wrapping around the root of his cock. "I am burning."

"You are drunk," I scold him. Drunk or drugged, there is little difference. Perhaps it would be fair play to repay him for the wrongs that have been done unto me, yet I cannot stomach the thought. Stealing from him what was taken from me will not return it.

"Look, Ruari. I weep for you." He trails his fingers through his pre-cum, then holds them out. They shine in starlight. I drop my gaze, cheeks aflame.

"Then weep alone."

It is a long night. Aries pleads for me in between bouts of pleasuring himself and I lose count of the number of times that he spills. His poor cock must be chafed and raw but still at first dawn, he is begging, his hand on his shaft and his eyes on me. Finally, as second dawn crests, his words slow. His body grows sluggish and sleep takes him.

I am left, untouched but yearning, to keep watch into the day.

Chapter Two

Rory

Aries slumbers.

I watch.

First, I watch the trees with their grasping limbs and shifting roots. Like all trees in Faerie, they are sentient but these...these feel wrong. Malignant, a malicious cancer churning in the dirt. They creep from their holes, changing the landscape until I can no longer pinpoint which direction we came from. At least I can still hear the slow-moving river.

Then, I notice the shadows. They quiver as if afraid, and stretch, contrary to their nature, toward the sun like they are begging for death. But it seems that even the sun has turned her face away from this wretched place.

Shuddering, I decide to stop watching the woods. Instead, I watch Aries.

In sleep, he is peaceful. His face is slack, having abandoned a tension I hadn't realized he carried. His right hand is still cradling his now-flaccid shaft while his left is splayed open on the damp soil beside his thigh. His left leg is outstretched but his right folds to the side, knee bent. The fabric of his pants is pulled taut, which only highlights his leonine frame. Corded with muscle but slender as a ballerino, nothing like the man I met in Old York what felt like years ago, or even the one who bedded me.

Ever since Aries first learned to glamour himself, he'd never stopped. He'd started small, adding a hand of height and half-a-cubit of breadth across his shoulders. On Earth, I'd noticed how he'd shortened his fingers by a joint — likely less for aesthetics and more for ease of firing his service weapon.

Now, glamourless, he is a familiar stranger. So like to the young boy who'd stalked me, ever-watching, from the cradle to the cot, and so different from the dark-eyed man who'd tumbled me into spider-silk sheets.

The second sun has completed over half her path when Aries begins to stir. It starts with a curl of his fingers. His elegant nails dig into the soil, creating little trenches before he flattens them back out. Then, he stretches out his leg toward me, coming close to touching mine. His eyes open with a flutter, his long eyelashes fanning twice before they stay open.

For just a moment, he looks at peace. Then, he tries to move his head. The vines still tangled around his rack hold him in place and tension floods back to his face. His whole body seems to stiffen and he finally, for the first time since we stumbled into the cradle knoll, releases his dick to clutch at his antlers instead.

How many times have I woken like that, pinned to the ground by weedy wildflowers and hair-twisting vines? Yet immediately, I find myself astride him, moving by instinct with no real direction from my brain. Pulling his grasping hands down, I replace them with my own, working quickly to free him now that he seems lucid enough not to pin me down and rape me.

I've nearly freed him before the thought comes to me to let him suffer like I have, but except for a brief hesitation, I continue working at the vines.

"Stop struggling," I urge him as he twitches and flinches beneath me, every movement threatening to buck me off.

At my words, he stills but it doesn't stop the low growl that rumbles from his chest. "What happened? Why am I bound like a pig for slaughter?"

"When have you ever bound a pig, Princeling? I've seen you hunt boar and never once stop to bind it," I tease, hoping it hides the way his deep, rumbling voice has affected me.

He is not moved by my amusement. Instead, his body is stonelike, statue-still beneath me. "Untie me," he orders, as if that's not what I am already trying to do. Perhaps it was meant to be a plea but it's demanding enough that this time, I do drop my hands, resting my weight back on his thighs with a frown.

"Do you think I am straddling you for fun, Aries? Perhaps I should leave you to free yourself, as you have me so many times." Angry now, I run my fingers through his crown of curls before I grip his hair to hold his head in place. Leaning closer, I meet his eyes with mine. "I would advise you, Princeling, not to tempt me now, while I am doing you a courtesy never once have you done for me."

Shame flashes dark in his eyes before fleeing. His throat moves as he swallows. He holds his head still and says, "Proceed."

"As you wish," I reply snidely and work, rather slower than I was before, on untangling the vines. I swear they feel slimy, slippery in my hands, though they appear to be bone dry. It is as if they don't want to release him. Or, perhaps, it is all in my head, my own hesitation manifest.

As soon as I see one of the vines snake back around an already freed tine, though, my hesitation vanishes and I finish freeing him quickly. Before I can scramble off him, though, he grabs my wrist with one of his large hands and plants his other on my waist, holding me in place.

"Explain," Aries demands. "Why did you place me in bondage?"

"I placed you in nothing, Princeling, but this knoll. You tangled yourself up all on your own." I yank my hands free and thankfully he lets me. If he'd resisted, I'd likely have succeeded only at damaging myself.

"I don't…" He stops, confusion on his face.

"Zephyr kicked you into the water," I explain, "and then you…" I stutter over the next words, dropping my gaze to his exposed cock instead. He follows it down with his own.

"Ah," he says, and his expression clears. "A Bourne of Aphrodisia." I have no idea what he means, and maybe he can see that on my face. He explains, "Running water that stirs a faerie's loins. The last one in Sidhe lands dried up before I was blossomed, but Arteria spoke wistfully of bathing in them and the orgies that would follow." Aries tucks his penis away and reties the closure of his pants, sighing. "Though perhaps these are not the same waters, because he never said anything about memory loss."

"He probably also didn't try to swallow the entire river at once. Still, I suspect nothing here is the same as we are used to," I mutter, looking out again at the changed woods. I am tired from a night and day of lost sleep but the thought of closing my eyes and lying down here…something tells me I would never stand back up.

I push myself to my feet and clamber out of the cradle knoll. "We should get moving."

"Zephyr?" Aries asks as he follows me out.

"He ran while I was dragging you from the river," I remind him, guilt swelling again though I do my best to stamp it down. I can't change the past and even if I could, there would be a dozen other things I'd change first.

Aries clamps his eyes closed and ducks his head but only for a second. Then he sighs and straightens up. "We cannot go back. If his breeding runs true, he will either find us again or return home to his stable." He looks around. "I do not know the way…"

"Listen for the river," I advise and start to head toward the sound.

Aries clamps his hand on my biceps and jerks me to a halt. "I hear it over here," he says, gesturing in the other direction.

"Well, fuck."

Chapter Three

Marik

The Queen is finally sleeping, leaving Marik free to slip out of her chambers. As has become typical, the corridor surrounding her rooms is barren of life. None want to risk her attention now. She's as likely to cast a curse as a blessing, but even her blessings have edges like knives.

Marik bypasses his office and his chambers to go straight to the hot springs. They are located on the lowest floor, at the mouth of the cave system the castle was formed over. The stone archway is narrow and the hallway dim, lit only by the faintly glowing moss clinging to its surface. The end of the corridor widens slowly until it opens into the cavern.

The walls have been worn smooth by the billowing steam and thousands of hands. Some faerie, his name lost to time, had carved elegant alcoves, complete with benches, right into the wall, two on either side of the entrance. Spidersilk curtains hang open on each one, swaying gently. The alcoves are empty.

Marik looks to the deep water. He barely lays his eyes on the two faeries, a silkie and a water nymph, before the pair is scrambling up the steps. They keep their eyes averted as they hurry past him to the exit, neither bothering to dress.

Once, Marik had been respected for his position. The Queen's left hand, second only to the Prince. Since Aodhan left — *though he goes now by Aries*, Marik reminds himself — love has turned to fear, respect to whispers at his back. Even Aries had looked at him with worry in his eyes and a hand on the hilt of his sword — Aries, his former friend. Aries, who had not even witnessed the horrors this place has turned him into.

They should be thanking him, all of them. For every moment he spends in her bed, another is spared. Instead, they curse his name and plot his downfall, as if he is not already prostrated for the Queen's amusement on a nightly basis. As if he does not ache by morning.

Pushing his anger away, he strips, leaving his clothing, abandoned, on the bench in the nearest alcove. Then, he unbraids his hair. With careful fingers, he frees each hidden bead. Two green, tucked into the center of the braid behind his left ear. Two white, near his crown. And one singular red bead — red as rubies, red as blood.

He tucks them neatly into his stockings. The dastardly things have a mind of their own, he knows, and left free to wander, he's as likely to find them in his nightly soup as where he left them.

Nude as a faeling, he walks to the edge of the shimmering pool and lowers himself into it. The water is hot as he sinks fully beneath the surface. For several moments, he does nothing but soak. Everything is quiet.

But as he sighs, his breath bubbling out, he hears it. The whispers of the water, muttering to him the secrets of all those who have come before him. Stolen from their sweat and tears, the hot spring has held onto them for Marik. Now, it shares them freely.

The kobold cook, she sent the Borrowed Boy away with a belly of tea and your most precious map. A secret, true, but one he knew. The mortal could not have stumbled out of the castle and into the Wilds without help and only Penny had a soft enough heart to aid him. Marik would turn a blind eye, as he's always done. He'd had the chance to return the boy and chose to let him slip through his fingers.

The water continues to babble — of blue-haired sprites and poisoned plots, of the elf with a dagger heart, and of the crying of the May-tree. It tells Marik of lesser gossip, too, like the pair of brothers who sneak into the Prince's garden, abandoned since his departure, to lay with each other under the light of the moon, and of the silkie who has snuck in a female, despite the Queen's law.

Marik will do nothing about either of those, though he tucks the information away for future blackmail. One never knows when a spot of intrigue will come in handy at Court.

As the last of the bubbles he'd exhaled pop, the water finally grows silent. Marik kicks his way to the surface and finds himself in the very heart of the hot spring. It is too deep for him to touch the bottom so he treads water. His feet, now webbed, stir up tiny waves around him. He swims toward the edge, to the shelf made of seashells built just above the water's surface. Grabbing a bar of harsh, jasmine-scented soap meant for laundry, he takes it to his skin.

It stings, then burns. When he finally feels clean, every trace of the Queen's poisonous fluids washed from his body, his skin is nearly scarlet. He returns the much smaller laundry bar to the shelf and grabs a blue glass bottle next. Tugging the cork free, he pours a small palmful of oil into his hand. He works it through his hair, lathering the lavender soap through every strand and into his scalp.

When he is ready to rinse, he pushes back from the wall and sinks under the surface again. The water, usually quick to cool his sore skin, does nothing to soothe him now.

Instead, he starts to itch. At first, he ignores it but quickly it grows more violent, like thousands of fire ants have burrowed beneath his skin. He scratches at his arms but succeeds only in opening bloody rivulets.

"Thorns!" he curses, pushing his way back to the edge of the hot spring and pulling himself out. He shakes the water free from his skin, staring incredulously at the welts left behind. Swiping a finger through the remaining dampness, he lifts it to his nose and sniffs.

"Salt?" he mutters, frowning as he shakes the droplet off. Now he can see it. The center of the hot spring, over where he assumed the wellspring cycled in new water, has grown cloudy. Tendrils like fingers crawl outward until the entire *onsen* is contaminated. He can smell the brine from where he stands.

The water is silent as a grave now.

* * * *

Rory

We find our way to the river not by listening for it. We can't even trust the shadows that twist and turn every which way. Instead, we follow the suns. They guide us to the shallow creek.

"It's too wide to jump," I say, and together we stare at it. Maybe Aries could jump it with his long legs and powerful thighs...but I still feel weak from my time spent drugged and pliable at the palace. The lack of food these past few days hasn't helped. Perhaps I could have jumped it once, during my days in Old York stealing bits and baubles.

I'd gathered some downed wood near the edge of the forest and shoved it into Aries' bag for firewood, but none of it would be long or thick enough to be helpful here.

I look around, hoping to see a log we can use as a makeshift bridge, but the forest is artificially pristine, every leaf and twig in place as if sculpted by some greater being. That alone is odd enough to distract me from our dilemma for a moment—long enough for Aries to grab me around the waist, his hands tight, and lift me.

"Brace yourself," he orders, but I've barely had time to process the words before he throws me. A scream tears from my throat. Wind digs through my hair and I see the black water coursing below me. I imagine it reaching up like hands to grab me and drag me below its surface, then I'm clear of it, slamming into the packed dirt on the opposite bank and rolling. My shoulder burns with pain and my hip aches where I landed on a sharp stone, drawing out another yelp.

For a second, I lie on the ground, stunned, before anger burns in my chest. I force myself up, glaring across the water at him. He is standing, hands on his hips, a smug smile on his stupid face. He takes a step back and crouches, clearly preparing to leap, and everything in me narrows in on him, focusing.

It would serve him right to land in the water. The bitter, caustic thought strikes me like a bell but I force it down. We can't afford to spend another night and day here while he works the aphrodisiac out of his system, not to assuage my anger.

He leaps. For a second, he is flying. His shirt billows as the wind snags it, flaring open like outstretched wings—an angel caught for a single moment in golden light. Then he lands and he is just a man again, staring at me with a smug smile.

"What?" he says, even his voice leaking arrogance. "It worked."

"Toss me again," I snarl, barely restraining myself from shoving him. "I *fucking* dare you." He may have landed safely on the bank, but it would only take a *little* push to send him stumbling backward into the water. I squeeze my hands into fists instead.

"Oh, lighten up, buttercup," he says, strolling past me without a care in the world. I grab his arm and drag him to a stop, my fingertips leaving trails of dirt on his skin. The mud, so dark against my pale flesh, is gray against his.

He could easily keep walking, tug himself free. I am weak compared to him. Instead, he stops. He looks down on me—always down—and lifts a brow. "Yes, my little hart?"

"I'm not a fucking deer," I argue, offended enough that it distracts me for a moment. Immediately, I continue with what I meant to say in the first place. "And I am no longer your meek little plaything to do with what you will. If you cannot treat me as an equal, then go back to your palace, Prince."

His smile stays for just a second before it fades. Sober, he straightens his shoulders. "My apologies,

Rory," he says, though it comes out forced, as if through gritted teeth. "I meant only to help."

"Your *meaning* does not matter as much as your actions," I say. Apologizing may go against his nature, but accepting it without question goes against mine. My gums are stinging as my monster's teeth threaten to drop. "I am not a doll, Aries. You would do well to remember this." I turn away.

I need to put some distance between us, but he follows on my heels. Always, he's been arrogant. It goes hand in hand with the crown he wears on his head, the stupid Circlet of the Forest Deer or whatever the fuck it is.

To be fair, he's been easier to deal with than I feared when I first spotted him with his little kelpie shadow. With few exceptions, he's almost seemed to have matured. Or at least, so I'd thought briefly before he pulled this stunt.

The anger seeps out of me slowly, though some still lingers. My shoulders slump. If he'd bothered to ask before he threw me, I might have agreed with his plan in the end. After all, I'd been nearly ready to give it up as a lost cause. I could see of no way across, short of felling a tree to form a makeshift bridge. I have no doubt that either his sword or mine could have easily accomplished it—their blades are sharper than diamonds. But in this forest, with its malicious aura...doing so might have signed our death warrants.

Simply crossing through her bounds has angered her enough.

So maybe I see why he did what he did. I still don't have to like it.

We must walk at least a furlong before I think I am calm enough to talk again. I stop at the crest of a low hill and stare at the expanse of forest still before us. For a second, I can pretend we are back in the Queen's Forest.

Aries steps up beside me. For once, he is silent, leaving it to me to speak first. I take in a breath. The air is crisp but strangely cold. I shiver, then rub my arms with my hands.

Finally, I sigh. We should have had this talk ages ago. "You don't understand what it was like for me, Aodh—Aries." Inwardly, I curse my slip of the tongue but he doesn't comment. He doesn't say anything. I continue anyway. "What it was—and still is—like for all of us Borrowed here."

A breeze blows my hair into my face. I brush it away. "You, all of you, were like…" I try to think of the right analogy, but all I can come up with is, "children with a brand new toy, and each one of you competing to see who could break theirs first."

He doesn't disagree.

I can't look at him. "Did you know I used to envy Aoife?"

"Didn't she…" he starts to say, his voice trailing off.

"Drown?" I finish for him. "Technically, though it wasn't an accident. She'd been talking about it for months. None of us thought she'd really do it though."

"She…" Aries swallows. I can hear it.

"Killed herself, yes. Waited until she saw the kelpie in the lake, then climbed astride him. We all watched her go under." I will never forget the smile on her face before the water went still.

"That wasn't an accident?" Aries sounds shocked and, if I'm not mistaken, offended. "Tadhg was banned from the lake for a fortnight."

"Oh, poor *Tadhg*." I roll my eyes. "All Aoife did was walk into the lake and wait for him. He came of his own free will."

"He nearly dried out!" Aries' voice gets louder.

I huff and throw a hand up. "Never mind. I should have known better than to think you'd listen." I start down the hill.

"Wait! I'm sorry, I'm listening," Aries says, grabbing for my arm. His hand barely touches my biceps when my foot hits a patch of slippery black mud and I start to slide. "Shit," Aries curses but his voice grows quieter as I move quicker. I manage to stay upright only for the first few feet before I tumble head over heels.

I land with an "*oof!*" at the base of the hill, in a patch of mud more like an oil-slick than anything else. For a second, I am breathless, but then I feel something moving in the mud and yelp, scrambling to my feet and onto the grass. I swear I can feel the clinging mud moving and I swallow down a gag.

Then Aries is there, swiping at the slick on my skin with the remains of what used to be his shirt.

"Get it off, get it off!" I'm crying and I don't know why. Living mud, hardly the worst thing I've ever had on my skin but for some reason, it's my tipping point today.

Maybe it's something in the mud.

Or, maybe, I was already on the cusp of a breakdown, trying to explain something to Aries that I don't think he'll ever understand.

"It's off, Rory. It's off," I finally hear Aries reassuring me and when I look, I see he's right, or mostly. All that is left is streaks.

Feeling silly, I pull away, or try to. Aries keeps hold of me, tugging me even closer to his chest. His bare chest, I can't help but notice, even now. "I'm fine," I say, though my voice is shaking. "You can let me go, I'm fine."

"No," Aries says, and his grip loosens just enough that if I wanted, I could have pulled away. For some reason, I stay still. "No, you're not fine. And you were trying to tell me that, weren't you? Seems I still haven't learned to listen."

"It doesn't matter anymore. It was a long time ago," I mutter, but even I know I'm lying.

"It does matter, Rory, because *you* matter. I'll do better at listening this time. Please, tell me what you were going to say." Aries guides me toward a large, flat-topped rock to the side of the trail. I eye it for anything unusual but it's just what it appears to be — a rock. He settles us on it, side by side.

My mouth is dry so I lick my lips. He holds out the bladder of water and I take a small sip, trying to conserve what little remains. Who knows if the water in this forest is safe to drink?

"You envied Aoife," Aries prompted. "It was that bad?"

I sighed, looking down at my dirty pants, then at the leaf-strewn ground. Anywhere but at him. "It may have been fun and games for you, but for us…Aries, it would have been kinder to line us up and slit our throats. Every day was…well, I don't have another word for it but torture."

Beside me, Aries flinches. He can't be surprised, he'd been there. An active part of most of it, and when he wasn't, at the very least a passive participant. Nothing happened without his knowledge. Not then, at least.

"Torture…" Aries repeats.

"Well, what else would you call it?" I finally force myself to look at him. "What we went through?"

Aries doesn't answer but his face shows his dawning understanding. I continue, "We didn't *age*, Aries. Not

28

like we should have. Our lives prolonged for...for... Gods, how to even gauge the time? Can you imagine being stuck in the body of a child while your mind grows older? Understanding that everything going on around you is wrong but being too weak to do anything about it?" My breath is shaky as I draw it in.

"But that is not the point. The point is...life really sucked. Enough that death...well, the ones who died seemed like the lucky ones." I lift a shoulder, feigning a careless shrug that is anything but. "Our lives were wholly dependent on the faeries we were bound to. You could have us killed, or beaten or...or raped, not that we even knew that word then, with the snap of your fingers. And you did, so many times."

"I *never* let them rape you," Aries protests, his voice hot.

"No, *you* didn't," I agree. "That was the line you drew for me. And perhaps I was not as grateful then as I should have been." It is a distinction that hardly matters to me now. Raped then or after, did it truly matter? But I can see that it matters to him. I keep talking.

"The others...not all of them were that lucky. You must realize that the threat was always there, in the back of my head. When were *you* going to cross that line?" Maybe he never would have. I hadn't known that at the time.

Aries stays silent.

"You didn't stop Anik from forcing us all into the dancing shoes."

Copper shoes shaped like ballet slippers with spikes in the heel, so when we fell — which we inevitably did — we'd be stabbed by sharp metal barbs. We'd danced for hours, tears sticky on our cheeks. But at least Aries had stopped them from heating mine in the fire.

"Or Anwynn and Alberich from rubbing hogweed in our eyes and abandoning us in the forest to find our way out."

Blinded, eyes burning and skin blistered, stumbling around naked for days. Aries had eventually found us but I still remember the sound of his laughter when he'd stumbled upon me in that clearing—and that he had left the others to find their own way out. I still wonder what happened to Nima. She'd never made her way home.

"I'd forgotten about that," Aries says softly.

"I didn't. I doubt any of us have," I reply. "What happened to the others, Aries? To Maeve and Una? To Oisin?" I knew of those who passed before I left, but not what happened to those who remained.

"I wish I knew." Aries looks genuinely upset by his answer, but it is exactly the one I expected him to give. Why would a faerie have lowered himself to ask after a mere human?

I sigh. "Old habits are hard to break, Aries. I know that. But there is only so much grace that I have within me to extend you." I stare out at the woods again. "I cannot be your doll again. I *will* not. I spent too long under your heel, and too long building myself back up into a semblance of a person, to go back to that now."

"I cannot promise that I won't make a mistake, it would be a lie. But I promise to try," Aries says, and it is the best I can hope for.

I shift on the stone to face him, then lift my hand to his chest, feeling the strong, steady beat of his heart. "Try hard, Aries. I am learning how not to hate you. It would be a pity if you were to ruin that."

Chapter Four

Rory

We sit in silence beside each other for several long minutes before I sigh and stand. Aries immediately follows, and when I look at him, he has a hangdog expression. The only thing he's missing is wringing hands.

I narrow my eyes. "I didn't tell you this so you would pity me, nor do I want to be the recipient of a guilt trip. Just...do better from now on, yeah?"

He nods but he doesn't look convincing. I have said all I mean to say on it. If he is uncomfortable with my words, they are his emotions to sit with. I swing the quiver around my shoulder and let it rest on my chest, fishing out the map. I unroll it, laying it on the flat top of the boulder we'd just been sitting on.

Aries holds down two of the corners for me without my having to ask. I skim my finger across the landmarks — the Queen's Forest, over the desert, and up to the Dead Woods we currently stand in. Then, I glance at the legend in the corner.

If it is accurate—and there's no telling it is, not without knowing who drew it and how long ago, or how much the forest has changed since—they cover a span of around four hundred furlongs—or about a thousand city blocks. I know from experience that I can cover roughly four hundred city blocks in a day if I push myself.

I run my finger over the vellum, tracing the intricately drawn woods. I let my finger stop about two-thirds of the way through, over what I think may be a river. "I think we should be about here… So maybe out by twilight?"

Aries leans over me, his breath skimming my ear, and looks as well. "This is one of Arteria's," he murmurs. He shifts his left hand from the corner to stroke along the lines. "So it's quite old. I think it would be safe to say that the forest has spread since then. Perhaps we should plan for tomorrow at the earliest, just to be safe."

"I do not wish to sleep in these woods," I admit, hesitating to put the map away, not with the way his fingers are stroking the vellum.

"No…but traveling at night is just as perilous. We should sleep in shifts." Aries pulls his fingers away and reluctantly I roll up the map, tucking it back into the quiver.

"Arteria?" I ask, my voice lifting at the end of what I assume is a name. It is familiar, sitting on the tip of my tongue though I can't pinpoint why.

"The commander of my mother's armies," he explains and immediately, I remember him. He'd been old, even by faerie standards, his hair the white of starlight. I'd seen him from a distance, but he'd never liked me, always sending me away when Aries had his training sessions. I sense, from the sorrow in Aries' voice, that he no longer walks in Faerie.

"I remember him," I say. "He was never cruel." It is the only homage I have for him. I believe there is more to being a worthy person than a lack of cruelty, but in Faerie, even that is a rare thing.

"No," Aries agrees. After a second of silence, he clears his throat. "We should keep moving."

I hum in agreement and start moving again, leaving the rock behind us. I am paying more attention to our surroundings, now that I know of the tricks the trees will play on us.

It is not the trees that come for us next.

Dusk falls gently around us but we don't stop quite yet. The ground is covered with sharp, glass-like gravel and neither of us wish to sleep upon it. Finally, as true dark starts to settle, I spot a faintly glowing clearing off the path to the right. "There!" I point toward it and Aries' gaze follows my finger.

"I suppose it's as good a place as any," he says, but he sounds hesitant. To be fair, I feel the same. It seems too easy, like the forest wanted us to find it.

But I will never know what plot the forest had planned to lay for us, because as soon as we enter the clearing with its softly swaying lavender grasses, I see it. A patch of wildly growing long-stemmed flowers. Moonlight glints off the vibrant purple petals and the silver leaves glow on their own — the source of the light we'd spotted.

If it had been any other plant, it may have been fine.

But it's not. At the sight of the *Salvia*, my stomach cramps and I gasp, clutching at my abdomen, gaze locked on the bulbs. It would only take one, just a taste…

I ignore Aries, who has crossed the grass to the center of the clearing and started unrolling our bedrolls. I note his actions only to make sure he won't stop me, grateful that he hasn't noticed my reaction yet. He'll stop me, I know it, take them for his own.

But I need it, just me. There is enough here to keep me sated for weeks or longer, but only if he doesn't take it from me. I should find a way to hide the bulbs from sight. Maybe, if I pick them quick enough…

But I don't have enough time. I've plucked the head from the first flower when Aries spots me. "Rory? What are you—"

I can't let him stop me. He will, I know he will. There's no time for me to hide the *Salvia* bed from him now, and he's already pushed himself to his feet, alarm on his face. If I want a taste, I can't wait.

I shove the flowers, as many as I can grab with two hands before he reaches me, into my mouth, my cheeks bulging out like a chipmunk, as I struggle to swallow. I gag at the slimy texture but the taste of mint hits me immediately.

Aries starts toward me and I growl in threat. I do not plan to share my spoils. He stops and lifts his hands, placating my anger, and I relax. As soon as I do, my vision goes fuzzy. I let myself fall back amongst the flowers and sigh, suddenly content.

Aries

By the time I spot Rory's strange behavior, it's too late to stop him. He tears at the flowers surrounding him, shoving them in his mouth like a starving beast, his eyes locked on mine. There's an intensity in them that I've seen before.

My kind rarely make good parents, and the species of Elyries who wanted to be often didn't get the chance. Barred from working all but the most menial jobs, constrained to the worst neighborhoods if they could get housing at all, denied entry to stores who didn't wish to affiliate with non-humans... Even the parents with the best of intentions were often forced to watch their children waste away.

Far too often during my stint at the BAA, I'd been sent into homes to remove children from their neglectful parents. I'd never forget their gaunt forms, their hollow cheeks and dull eyes — the way they'd looked at me like they were waiting for another strike.

Rory looks at me just like that now.

I start toward him, hoping to get him to spit out whatever plants he'd consumed so eagerly but he gives me a vicious growl, the threat clear. *Come closer and I'll bite.*

I stop, holding up my hands in hopes of calming him, surprised when it works. Too easily he relaxes, then falls backward into the bed of flowers. Carefully, I creep toward him but now he is ignoring me completely.

I freeze when I reach his side, staring down at the shredded petals sticking to his fingers with horror as soon as I recognize them.

Salvia.

I fall to my knees. When had Rory, my sweet Rory, gotten hooked on *Salvia*? Only an addict would have spotted the flowers so quickly. They weren't of themselves all that alluring. They have no scent to beckon one in, not like the strange glowing hearts we'd spotted when we'd first entered the Dead Woods.

No, Rory's reaction can only be explained by former exposure.

Salvia... It is a hell of a drug. More addictive than heroin, I'd always been grateful it had fallen out of favor at court and later, once I became an agent, even more grateful it had never made its way to earth. Pimps would kill for it. All the addictive properties of a street drug but with the added bonus of complete compliance. And the whole time they were under the influence, users would be blissfully happy.

Salvia sluts would make the perfect prostitutes.

"Fuck," I curse out loud, sitting down abruptly as my legs threaten to give out. Agony clamps around my chest like a vice as I stare at his blissed-out form.

Like this, he looks young again, the weight of hard years stripped from his shoulders. His eyes are open but distant and there's a smile on his face that I've never seen. For just a second, I see the draw — how many times in the past had I wished to see him look at me like this? Like all is right in the world and he is truly happy, unburdened by a single care?

As soon as the thought crosses my mind, I stamp it down, ashamed. I want him happy, but not like this. Never like this.

"Who did this to you, sweet hart? Who turned you out?" I murmur, reaching over to brush his curls out of his eyes. He doesn't answer. I hadn't expected him to. He does shift slightly, turning his face into my palm. Along his jaw is the beginnings of red scruff, not quite a beard but definitely more than I'm used to on him. In my memories, his skin is always fresh and smooth — he hadn't even needed to shave.

I can't resist stroking my fingers over its velvet softness before, reluctantly, I pull my hand free. It's not fair to touch him like this, not when he can't say no, I know that. How many hundreds of hours of sensitivity training had I sat through at the Bureau? How many experts had been brought in to teach myself and my fellow fae about consent?

Instead, I shake his shoulder. "Angel?" I say, wondering if, since Rory is out of it, I can convince him to wake up instead.

Rory just blinks at me and smiles. Apparently, the *Salvia* works on both aspects of him. That will make this harder, but not impossible. We can't stay here, not if I want to sober him up anytime soon. Who knows how long the flower will remain in his system with as much as he's swallowed?

Leaving him in the bed of flowers, I quickly pick up our bedrolls and pack them away again, swinging my bag over my shoulder before I return to him. "Come on, sweet hart. Stand up for me."

Obediently, he pushes himself to his feet, humming under his breath as he sways from foot to foot. We start to walk but I realize quickly how distracted he is. As soon as I take my eyes off him, he wanders off the path or drops to his butt, dragging his fingers through the dirt like a child, giggling all the while.

Maybe he will hate me for it later but I can't risk losing him in the dark. I scoop him into my arms, cradling him to my chest as I carry him along the path. He drops his head against my shoulder, his fingers fiddling with the collar of my shirt. He's still humming a tune I've never heard before but he seems content enough to let me carry him.

I used to think that I wanted him docile—now that he is, I realize how much I hate it. He might look like Rory, but he's little more than a shell. A living, breathing doll. Exactly what he told me he never wanted to be again.

Fuck.

Chapter Five

Rory's Monster

I feel like I am swimming through a sea of honey. The air is thick and heavy, settling on Rory's face like a wet blanket, and it is hard to breathe. His mouth is fuzzy when I open it, and when I try to lift his arms, they feel as if they have been filled with lead.

I sense no danger, feel no injuries. Why have I surfaced instead of Rory? I try to ask him, but he is sleeping somewhere deep inside. My words aren't reaching him. Reluctantly, I blink open his eyes, wincing at the too-bright sky. Tears sting our lashes.

I press our eyes closed until the brightness seems tolerable, then open them again, struggling to look around. My head pounds like someone is beating the inside of my skull with a hammer.

What the hell happened?

Rory's body is curled up on a rumpled bedroll, his back pressed against something cold and hard. When I twist around to peer over our shoulder, I see that it is a boulder. The move pulls at sore muscles so I stop craning, staring across from us instead.

There, leaning against the moss-covered trunk of a sleeping tree, is Aries. He is awake, or at least his eyes are open. His head is cast back, his eyes on the sky.

I try to talk but all that comes out is a dry, strangled croak. Immediately, Aries' gaze drops to meet mine.

"Rory?" he asks, leaning forward.

To his credit, he doesn't look as disappointed as I fear—though why it matters to me, I don't know and refuse to evaluate—when I shake my head. I wonder what I look like now. Clearly, I haven't fully taken over, if he's mistaken me for my host.

"What happened? Why am I awake and Rory is...not?" It's happened before but fewer times than I could count on one hand.

Something twists Aries' face, an emotion I can't recognize. I can read violent intent and anger, sometimes lust...but the rest are harder for me to place. He answers my question before I've put a name to the feeling, and I let it go.

"Rory stumbled on a flower before I saw it and ate it," Aries explains.

Immediately, I understand. Now, the stale mint in my mouth makes sense. "*Salvia.*" I spit, trying to clear out the taste.

Aries nods. "I wasn't sure if you remembered it or not, it seemed to affect you just as much as he, if not more. I couldn't rouse you."

I crinkle my nose in disgust. "Unfortunately. I have no control over his body when he's under its influence but as his memories return, I share them. It's a nasty drug."

"Yes, it is," Aries agrees.

For some reason, that surprises me. "Your brethren seem to find it amusing."

"I am not my brethren," Aries responds, eyes flashing. *Danger,* they say. But I've never been great at listening to cautionary tales.

"No," I purr in agreement, forcing Rory's body upright, "you're not." It takes all my strength to prop us against the boulder in a way that doesn't look weak. Should I flirt with him? Give him what they all want before he thinks to take it? There's something in his eyes that convinces me it would be a bad idea.

"Did you sleep?" I say, noticing the bags under his eyes, so dark they look like bruises.

"I've been keeping watch," he says instead of answering directly.

I glance at the sky. The first sun is gone, the second descending toward the horizon. The *Salvia* has kept us under for most of the day.

"There's little point in moving on now," I decide. "You should get some rest and we can continue in the morning. Perhaps Rory will wake by then."

"You need your rest more," Aries says, but his words are split by a yawn.

"It's too bright. We can sleep in shifts." I expect him to argue further, but he must be more tired than I expect because after a moment, he gives a stilted nod and settles down on his bedroll. I shift my weight against the stone and wait for Rory to wake.

It's going to be a long night, I think, as I feel the first, far too familiar, cramp knotting Rory's stomach.

* * * *

Rory

I come back to myself in stages.

First, I feel the pain. The throbbing headache, the heartburn, then the sunburn-sensitive skin, all twisted together beneath a fever-like heat. My mouth is arid and tastes foul, like mint and vomit.

"*Finally*," my monster drawls, his voice as dry as my throat. "*I thought you would make me suffer your withdrawals forever.*" He starts to retreat back inside me.

Before he can, however, I call out to him, "*Wait! What happened?*"

"*I think this time, I'll leave you to pick up the pieces on your own. It is, after all, your own mess.*"

And then he is gone. Cursing inwardly at my useless passenger, I look around for clues. Aries is sleeping on a bedroll across from me, and my monster…must have been keeping watch? We are just off the path in a space too small to be called a clearing. It is the blue-dark of early morning, and I guess it is shortly before dawn.

I don't remember stopping—until I do. Suddenly, it all flashes back to me. The clearing, the *Salvia*…running my fingers across Aries' chest as he carries me away from the flower bed.

Making a fool of myself, though perhaps not as big of one as I could have, all things considered.

Fucking Salvia.

I hate that it's infected me again, especially since this time, there's no one to blame but myself. How long will this moment of lucidity last? Long enough for us to escape the woods? Or have I gotten lucky and I am through the worst of it by now?

There's no way to know for sure. Every time they'd force fed it to me, the comedown had been different.

Oh, the physical symptoms are always the same — the pain and cramping, the hot flashes and cold sweats — but the rest? The hallucinations, the voices...I can never predict them.

For all I know, this whole trip has been one long, drawn out hallucination and I'll wake up in the Queen's bower again, skin flayed from my skeleton, face carved into a smile.

There's no point dwelling on could-bes and maybes.

As the first sun rises in the sky, I stand and pack up my bedroll, then cross the small patch of grass to shake Aries awake. "It's time to move on," I tell him, trying to keep my voice even. I hope he doesn't ask me any questions.

He must read the reluctance on my face because after a brief hesitation, he nods and packs up his bedroll in silence. He doesn't talk until we are back on the path. "Rory?" he asks.

I wait for a question but none come. Then, I realize that he must have spoken to my monster while I was...sleeping. I wish I knew what they spoke of.

"It's me," I tell him.

"If you want to talk about—" he starts to say, and I interrupt him, walking faster so I don't have to meet his eyes.

"I don't."

"Okay. But if you do...I'm here."

It is surprisingly comforting.

Chapter Six

Rory

We don't walk as far as I'd hoped. Twice we have to stop when my body starts to shake too badly for me to keep going, and once more when I'm overtaken by a wave of nausea that leaves me slumped over just off the path, violently emptying the little contents that remain in my belly. Overall, it is a miserable day and even more miserable night. No matter how close to the fire I lie, I am freezing.

By the next morning, the worst of it seems to have passed and finally, I start to notice our surroundings again. The trees here are taller than ever. I hope it means that we are nearing the outer edge and not just now reaching the forest's heart. When I look toward Aries, he is frowning.

Everywhere I look, I see vibrant green exotic plants of every shape and color, growing brighter and bolder the deeper we walk. It is far from the dreary, desolate expanse near the outskirts. Even the woods we'd just been walking through, so pretty at first, seem dull in comparison. It is so pristine that at first, I don't notice the silence.

It yawns into existence around us, soft at first, like the quiet of a held breath. Then deeper, the still before a storm. Even our footsteps—mine first, then Aries at my side—are muffled, the sound swallowed by something in the shadows. It quickly becomes oppressive. I can hear every pounding beat of my heart, every rushing flow of blood through my veins, but outside my body? Nothing. It is as if my ears are stuffed with cotton. I dig at them with my pinkies but all I succeed at is scratching my ear canal.

My yelp is certainly loud enough.

"Shh," Aries hisses, grabbing my shoulder and forcing me to a halt, his chest pressing up tight to my back. He snakes his other arm around me, flattening his hand against my belly.

My breath catches.

We stand together, silent. His attention may be entirely on the surrounding woods, but mine is fixed on the warm heat of his palm and the way his lips skim along my neck and ear.

When he finally steps back, I feel lost. I want to ask him so many questions, but now that he's pointed it out, I feel something watching us. Drawing attention to ourselves seems dangerous.

For the first time since we entered this portion of the woods, I realize what is missing. For as long as we've been walking this morning, I've been admiring the vibrant fronds sprouting from the slender, bendy tree trunks, and the near neon brilliance of the flowers, questioning again why anyone would name a place so full of life the Dead Woods.

Until now, I'd been thinking that perhaps it was given its name because of the killer fruit or the water meant to enchant and distract, and maybe that is a part of it.

As we stand here, silent and still, I realize that, despite how lively the plants appear, I haven't seen a single creature, not a bird or a beast. And looking closer at the grass, there's not a bent blade in sight and no animal tracks either.

I step back into Aries. He steadies me with his hands. Softly, I whisper, "It's too quiet…"

Aries slaps his hand over my mouth but it's too late—as soon as I finish speaking, the forest explodes to…not life, but I'm too stunned to think of the right word. All I see before Aries shoves me to the ground and plasters his body to my back like a shield is a maelstrom of corpses. Some new, their bodies barely bloated, some rotted, and some little more than a shamble of bones.

I try to lift my head, unwilling to lie here silent in the dirt while dead things try to kill me, but Aries shoves my head down, hissing in my ear, "Stay still." I can barely hear him over the moaning and rattling and about the time I process his words, the stench of death hits me.

I gag and if it weren't for the way Aries has my face pressed into the grass, I'd probably vomit. The earthy smell of wet dirt masks just enough of the rot to keep the bile from rising. Something moves near me, close enough that blades of grass shift and poke into the exposed skin of my neck. I slam my eyes closed.

The childish mentality takes over — if I can't see them, they won't see me. Maybe it's not accurate — bad things always manage to find me, even when I can't see them, *especially* when I can't. The dark has always held nightmares.

My lungs strain until I have no choice but to draw in a breath. Air whistles into my lungs and for a second, the cacophony gets louder. Then, finally, it starts to calm. I feel the ground rumble and Aries loosens his grip.

Carefully, I lift my head. The ground is a mangled mess of churned dirt, but there is no sign of the remains. I'm afraid to move, a primal fear that I can't shake even as I realize that it is something *other*, imposed on me from an external source. The corpses, maybe, or maybe from the woods themselves.

I have questions — so many questions — but I'm terrified to make a sound. If we stand, will that be enough to draw them back to us? Aries must worry as well because he is still plastered to my back, his hands encircling my wrists in too-tight grip. I don't mind the bite of pain, not in this situation.

Zombies.

Fucking zombies.

Aries

I know I should move, should let Rory stand, but my body is frozen. I'd come so close — *too* close — to losing him. There's a phantom of a memory tickling the back of my mind, like I've felt this bone-deep horror before, but I don't know why.

My body is shaking but his is still, frozen beneath me. I let his wrists go, fingers unclamping with all the grace of an arthritic's, and run my hands down his arms to his sides, feeling the shallow quick breaths. He's alive, but is he conscious? Is he unharmed? I can't tell with the way his face is buried in the dirt.

Oh, shit. Am I smothering him?

Hesitant to make a noise but too worried not to check, I scramble off him as carefully as I can, turning him onto his back. He's conscious all right, his face pale but streaked with dirt, his green eyes wide. I press a finger to his lips to forestall any attempt at talking, then look him over.

His wrists are red from the tight grip I'd held them in but other than that and his scuffed elbows, he appears unharmed. I sag in relief, then sit back. Glancing around first to make sure there are no more of the corpses hanging around, I finally convince myself to stand. Slow as I can, I pull Rory up with me.

His foot lands on a twig. It snaps loudly in the otherwise silence and we both freeze. Mercifully, the forest stays still. Rory is clinging to me, his fingers digging into my skin and while it may be painful, it's another sign that he's alive. It's also interesting to me that here, in a moment of danger, he's holding onto me for safety. Maybe he doesn't trust me yet, not wholly…but at least part of him does.

I cup his cheeks, angling his head up until his gaze meets mine, and try to convey with my eyes a silent promise to keep him safe. I don't know if he understands completely but enough of my meaning must come through for him to relax. Slowly, he lets go of my arms. I snag his hand and interlace our fingers before he can back away completely, then carefully start to creep across the meadow toward the trees.

I don't know if the corpses were just in this clearing or if there are more of them and I have no desire to find out, so I am careful. My Boots of Wander might silence my footsteps but, unfortunately, they do nothing to help Rory. The second time he breaks a twig and we both freeze, I know that this won't work.

I tug him to a stop. Remembering how angry he got when I acted without asking last time, I try to mime my next steps. He frowns, but I think he understands. His teeth dig into his lip for a second and he looks torn but finally, he nods.

I scoop him up into my arms. He fits against my chest as if he was made to be there. And better yet, though he looks unhappy, he allows me to carry him out of the clearing and deeper into the woods.

Progress.

Chapter Seven

Marik

Marik does not bother to caution others of the spring. If they cannot smell the salt before they enter its depths, then they deserve to feel its bite on their skin. Instead, he goes to the stables. He makes quick work of saddling Aphid. The first get of the Queen's pride mare, Orchid, she is fast as a winter avalanche, and her gait is as smooth as a mountain hare.

She does not have her dam's endurance but when it comes to speed, she has no match. He's not sure where his sudden urgency is coming from, but something tells him he needs to move quickly.

There is something he needs to see.

Marik rides her out to the Black Road. As always, she hesitates for just a moment before stepping onto the hard, dark surface. Asphalt, they called it on Earth, or so he'd heard. While it certainly makes traveling easier, he can't help but feel there is something wrong about seeing its unnatural smoothness here.

What kind of world is Earth that its inhabitants have stripped the trees and grass and waters to replace it with this dead rock? He is one of the few faeries who has never visited the strange place, bound to the Queen's lands by the force of her will. He doesn't understand the allure so many others have with it.

This asphalt is unnatural, a blight on the natural world. Marik suspects Faerie agrees with him — she has pulled the wild grass back from either side, leaving only dry, dead dirt behind.

He nudges Aphid with his heels and, after her initial leeriness, she speeds up, her gait smoothing out. Thankfully, they don't have far to go. While the Queen's lands spread far and wide, her castle has always sat near to the May-tree.

Aphid slows as they approach the knoll she grows on. Marik swings off, dropping her reins. She won't wander far. He raised her from a foal, hand-fed her oats and strings of moonlight.

He starts up the side of the hillock, moving slowly. There's something strange about the grass... He is nearly halfway up before he realizes what it is.

The filaree are watching him.

Each broadleaf weed's hairy stalk is now topped with small, pupilless, unblinking eyes. They sway, spinning slowly to follow his path as he climbs. Shuddering, he looks away. There is something off-putting about the cloudy humanoid irises, above and beyond their existence in the first place. Yet another unnatural thing to add to his growing list of oddities. He reaches the top of the hill unharmed but wary.

Perhaps he should have been more concerned.

The May-tree is twisted beyond recognition.

Literally so, her trunk spiraled and crooked, limbs dragging toward the ground as if weighed down. Her leaves, once snowy-white, then purple and cankered, are now the crimson of Autumn — impossible, here in the land of undying spring. And where her knots of May should be, instead now hang golden globes the size of Marik's fist. They pulse slowly in time with his heart.

And worst of all, worse even than the bloody sap streaking her bark, is the crumpled body of the hamadryad at her base. None have ever laid eyes on the spirit of the May-tree, though many have tried, but instinctively, Marik knows that this used to be her. He feels it in his core.

Horror twines around his chest like catbrier. Her body is desiccated and mottled by sores, her face literally rotted away, leaving behind nothing more than tooth and bone. He'd known the tree was dying, but without knowing what ailed her, he'd had no means to help. Now, it is too late.

Whatever thing now grows on this hillock — because the crooked tree is still very much alive — it is no longer the May-tree. And while it does not speak to him, he feels its oozing maleficence in his very bones.

* * * *

Rory

Somehow, we make it to the edge of the woods alive. I can hardly believe it as we step past the last of the trees and I see the smudged suggestion of a lake in the distance. Suddenly, my mouth is as dry as a desert.

"We made it," I whisper, still afraid to make too much noise this close to the forest at our back.

"Not yet," Aries says, his own voice not quite as optimistic.

I swat his shoulder. "Stay positive. We're *going* to make it." I wiggle out of his arms and start walking toward what must be the loch from the map. "Are you coming?" I ask him over my shoulder.

He shakes his head but walks after me. "I'm not letting you go on your own," he answers. "Especially since the map was pretty damn vague about what we're walking into."

"A lake," I reply, though I know that's not what he means. "Usually," I clarify. "Or it could be a sea inlet, but that's unlikely this far from the ocean."

"I *know* what a loch is," Aries says, hustling a bit to reach my side. "But after the Black Blizzard in the desert and the shitshow back in the woods, I suddenly find myself suspicious of this so-called 'loch'."

I can't say he's wrong to be leery. "Well, whatever it is, I just hope the water is potable." I'd drunk some pretty nasty things living on the streets of Old York but there, the most I had to worry about was pollutants and microbes. Here in Faerie? Who could say what it could do to a person, especially a mortal one.

Unfortunately, I'll have to take my chances. Dehydration is not the way I want to go. Not that I want to go in *any* way. I'm no longer suicidal.

"Tell me something," I abruptly order him. Anything to get my mind off the dark place it's suddenly gone to.

"Like what?" he asks.

"I don't know. Anything," I answer. At this point, he could tell me a story about ordering Thai food, and I'd take it. Although maybe not, since I'm starving and a nice plate of khao soi would hit the spot just right. "Tell me how you ended up in that alley?"

A memory of the day I saw him again for the first time in centuries floats to the surface of my mind. Oh, he'd looked damn fine in his dark leathers. The wave of attraction, even more than the rush of terror that had immediately followed at seeing him again, had pissed me off. I'd been about to flee when he'd stumbled to his knees, catching himself with a bloody hand against one of my murals. And carelessly broken the geas I'd painted into it at the same time.

Remembering the heavy weight of those jagged emotions pouring back into me now, he's lucky I didn't leave him to bleed out. I'd certainly considered it.

"It's not a happy story," Aries warns me.

"Most faerie stories aren't," I remind him.

"I suppose you're right," he agrees. "The short version is—"

"Oh, come on," I interrupt him. "Are we on some sort of time crunch I don't know about? We have at least a half-day's walk, if not longer. I think you can tell the whole story."

Aries stares at me for a second, then sighs. "If you insist."

"Oh, I think I do."

"You know I work—worked—for the Bureau of Arcane Activity?" he asks.

It had taken me longer than it should have to place the logo on his leathers. I'd known he was a cop, but all law officers were the same to me—the worst were bullies and perverts, and at best they were apathetic.

I don't say any of this. I just nod, because I *had* placed it eventually. "The uniform *was* hard to miss."

"I suppose it was," he agrees. "Whoever designed them certainly wasn't going for stealthy." He grins, but the expression quickly fades. "Well, part of my job was investigating crimes involving Elyries. Anyone non-human," he explains, but I wave him on. I lived on Earth long enough to know what they were.

"So," he continues, "it all started with these portals. Someone was burning septagrams into the ground all over the city, opening pathways to Kur and unleashing demons. They were all low-level. Stupid and easy to contain, at least at first, even if they were running amok throughout the city. At first, we thought we could handle it. Then the summoner started calling higher level demons, and he was summoning them more and more often. When they started sending my agents to the hospital, I knew it was time to call in a..." Aries hesitates, then seems to decide on a word. "Specialist."

He swipes his palm over his head, barely avoiding his antlers. I like how his hair is growing out now, no longer the closely shorn black stubble it was when we met each other again. It's long enough to curl. It makes him look younger, less stoic.

"His name was Leviathan, and he was my friend," Aries says, pulling me back into his story.

I trip over my feet. "Leviathan? The *Blood* Demon?"

And I'd thought *my* demon roaming around the city, unchecked and undocumented, was bad enough.

"You've heard of him?" Aries sounds surprised.

"Heard of him? Of course I have! You'd have to be living under a rock not to have! Or worse, since for a few years I basically *did* live under a rock." I almost get distracted thinking about my days crashing under the Brooklyn Bridge with a half-troll named Benny, before I shake my head with exasperation. "Everyone knows about the Blood Demon. I was just always relieved to know he was safely away in Brekkan. Fuck, it's only a matter of time before the bastards go bonkers."

I'd heard the stories about the other ones, and the horrors they'd unleashed on the world before they'd been dragged back to Kur. And not, I always found it important to note, by any mortal creature. No, the only one who'd ever succeeded at putting one of them down had been an even *more* scary monster, the ruler of Kur himself.

"He didn't just...go bonkers," Aries argues. His dark eyes flash with anger and he clenches his fists. He draws in a breath as if to calm himself before adding, "He was helping the Bureau track the wix responsible for the portals. Everything that happened after? It was my fault for calling him in. Nobody would have died if he'd stayed on his estate in Brekkan."

"You're not responsible for his bad decisions. You asked him for help. I'm positive that you didn't tell him to destroy the whole city," I say. I shiver a bit at the memory of the Blood Storm and the casualties that followed.

Aries clenches his jaw and looks away, staring resolutely at the horizon.

It's clear he's not going to continue, so I bite the bullet and apologize. "Okay, I'm sorry. I guess I don't know the whole story. Please keep going?" He stays silent until I touch his arm. His skin is warm. "Please?"

His jaw twitches but he finally relents. "Leviathan was helping us, and we were getting closer to finding the culprit. Unfortunately, the bastard found him first. He stabbed Leviathan in the heart with a tourmaline stake, then stole his bonded, a werewolf named Eryn, while he was paralyzed. My superior was certain that

Leviathan would be uncontrollable if we released him, so she ordered me to hold him in containment while we searched for Eryn."

I wince. "Oh…oh, that's a terrible idea." To be fair, I have the benefit of hindsight, but even the jail cells I'd been thrown into a time or ten had barely contained me, and no one who'd met a real demon would think my monster was particularly threatening.

"Yeah. It was," Aries agrees. "To be fair, the prison was supposed to be impregnable. No one in and no one out without authorization. The Blood Storm? That's how he escaped. He tore through all his magic, even cannibalized his blood bonds, to get the energy to break through the wards. Doing that had…side effects, you could say. So you see, it wasn't his fault. It was mine."

I stop walking, hearing the pain in his voice, and grab for his hand. He pulls it away and steps back, avoiding my gaze. "I ended up in that alley because I couldn't bear the thought of killing him. I had the chance to shoot and the bullets in my gun to do it. Even after all the people he killed, my fellow agents, my friends…I hesitated. And he didn't."

I don't know what to say.

I can see it now, how every puzzle piece fell together to create the perfect storm of circumstances, but I could also see why he had made every decision that he had. I still didn't think it was his fault. He'd been following orders, and I doubt letting the demon run around the city unfettered would have led to a better option.

"I regret nearly every choice I made. But at the same time…" He meets my eyes again. "They led me back to you."

"I'm sure you're thrilled," I say dryly, though inwardly I feel like I'm flying. I try to shove the feeling away. I can't let myself be drawn back into his orbit, not when we will have to part ways at the Unsidhe border. "You're back in Faerie and on the run from Mommy. Oh, and trying not to get eaten by zombies. It's been a real vacation."

"You know, I'm rather enjoying myself," Aries says and I stumble again.

He can't lie.

"You find the strangest things amusing." It's either say that or kiss him, and if I let myself cross that line now, I know I won't want to stop, and we're still too close to the woods to linger for anything less than life-threatening.

"Or maybe it's just worth it to see you again." He's smiling, but it fades slowly into something gentler. "It *is* good to see you again, Rory. Less than ideal circumstances or not."

"I'm glad you're here with me," I admit.

Chapter Eight

Aries

The loch shimmers in the distance. We'd veered toward the Northwest shore in hopes of cutting off some travel time circumventing it. I doubt there will be a boat conveniently waiting for us. I don't know what I was expecting, but a coastline softened by silver sand and water as clear as glass certainly isn't it. It is the loveliest beach I've ever laid eyes on, more so even than the waters of my mother's land.

I stop Rory with an outthrust arm before he can step from the craggy grass. Things here are rarely what they seem, and I do not trust its beauty. Crouching, I brush my fingers through the sand. Nothing happens, so I wait a second before plunging my hand further in.

It is soft and warm and I feel nothing strange.

Rory, surprisingly, waits for me to stand and say it's okay before he steps forward. We both approach the water slowly. Again, he waits for me while I dip my fingers beneath the surface. And again, nothing happens.

I am beginning to suspect that the loch is just a loch.

We refill our water skin, then after a brief discussion, agree to rest here until morning. Neither of us are excited about the thought of climbing the foothills in the dark.

I pitch the tent while Rory pulls one of the bundles of firewood he'd collected in the woods—dry as bone, so it should be easy to burn—out of my bag.

"What are the odds the loch has fish in it?" Rory asks once he's finished lighting a small fire a few feet from the tent.

"I don't see any reason it wouldn't," I admit and grab my bag from him, digging around for a net. I don't find it—it's been so long since I packed this bag, my memory of adding one could be faulty—but I find some fishing line. Carefully spun from shed kelpie hair, using it requires careful handling. But, if done right, it works like no other.

Ignoring Rory's protest that he didn't mean I had to try, I slip out of my shirt and pants, leaving them on the sand. I don't think I'm imagining Rory's small gasp from behind me but, hiding my smile, I don't look back. Naked, I wade out until the sun-warmed water reaches my waist.

Keeping hold of one end of the line, I trail the other through the water until I've created a half-dozen steadily growing ripples. There's no need for bait—the line will take care of that on its own.

The sand is soft on my feet and the sun is warm on my skin and, slowly, the tension I seem to always carry seeps out, disappearing into the water. I feel my body relaxing.

Then, the line jerks.

I smile.

Looks like we will be having dinner after all.

I carry my catch back to shore and dress, my skin still damp.

It doesn't take long to scale, trim, gut and fillet the school of rainbow oarfish. It takes longer for Rory to find a smooth and flat stone large enough to prop in the fire to cook them on. Still, they are ready to eat before the sky is fully dark.

Twilight settles around us.

The fish are nothing special. Cooked without seasonings or butter, unkissed by the hands of our kobold cook whose magic adds unimaginable flavor, but still, I savor the taste. Is it better because for the first time in ages, I caught it with my own hands? How long has it been since I've cooked anything outside of a microwave?

I can hardly remember.

"This is really good," Rory sounds surprised. He's holding one of the extra flat stones as a plate, picking at the white meat with his fingers. "With a bit of salt, would be—" He lifts his fingers to his mouth and mimes a chef's kiss.

I laugh. "For you, maybe. But I suppose it could do with some pepper. Why do you sound so surprised?"

"Didn't know you could cook," Rory explains around his next mouthful.

"Didn't have much reason to, before," I answer. "I picked up a bit back on Earth. Didn't always make sense to go out, and take-out gets boring after a while."

"Was it weird for you? Food on Earth, I mean?" Rory asks.

"Yeah." I laugh, remembering the first time I'd eaten. The odd, plastic taste, the stinging of the chemicals on my tongue. I'd panicked enough to make myself sick. Thankfully, I'd still been staying at the halfway house for new arrivals and another faerie had been there to explain that it wasn't poisoned. "I can't say I miss the food."

"I don't know. I think I *will* miss some of it. Salted caramel, salted toffee, taza chocolate..." Rory moans at the end and my dick hardens.

"I'm noticing a pattern," I say as I try to subtly adjust myself.

Rory's gaze lingers on my hand, but he just smirks, then plops another piece of fish into his mouth. "You don't know what you're missing. Salt is food of the Gods."

I shudder at the thought. I've ingested it before, of course. Living on earth and eating take-out had made it nearly impossible not to. No matter how many times you ordered food without it, some idiot somewhere messed something up—either forgot that the butter was pre-salted or didn't check the label on the sauce bottle. It was another reason I'd learned to cook for myself.

Salt wouldn't kill me, but it certainly wreaked havoc on my intestinal track.

"I miss popcorn," Rory says. "Do you think there's a way to make it here?"

"I've never thought of it. Wouldn't hurt to try someday." I make a note in my mind to commune with Faerie soon. Popcorn shouldn't be out of her wheelhouse.

"Someday," Rory says, but he sounds sad. I realize why immediately. We don't have a 'someday' waiting for us. Once we get to the Unsidhe borders, he'll be leaving me.

Not me, I tell myself. *He's not leaving* me. *He's just…leaving. So he can be safe…away from me.*

For some reason, the distinction doesn't make me feel any better.

I look across the shining water to the other side, at the mountains that look like little more than smudged shadows against the darkened sky. How long will it take us to cross them? Two days? A sennight? Then he'll be gone, beyond my reach. And beyond my protection if anything goes wrong.

It is a fear that I've been struggling to ignore. The king of the Unsidhe is a mystery to me. I have seen him before but only from a distance, and we have never spoken. Unlike my Queen-Mother, he is not one of the high fae. Rather, he is a Fomorian. I remember the one and only time I saw him before I fled Faerie. He was tall enough he could not pass beneath the castle gate without stooping, and it topped out at ten feet at its center. His two curling black goat horns had lent him another foot of height. I don't recall much else about him except the man-sized sword strapped to his back.

"Want the last one?" Rory asks, pulling me from my thoughts as he gestures at the final fish crackling on the firestone.

"It's all yours."

Rory carefully works it onto his plate. Then, he tears it apart with his fingers and stuffs it into his mouth as if he hadn't already downed four of them. Pride burns in my chest—that he is eating food I caught, food that I cooked.

And he likes it, I can tell from the little moans he's making and the way his teeth have sharpened seemingly on their own.

I settle back on the warm sand with a contented sigh, folding my arm behind my head like a pillow as I stare at the dark sky. Rory sets his makeshift plate aside and lies beside me.

"There are no stars," he comments and I hum in agreement.

"Faerie has no stars. There are no other galaxies here, not like on the mortal plane," I explain.

"But I've seen them before, many times. Lying in the moss in your garden....by the little lake outside the castle walls..." Rory turns to stare at me and I meet his gaze. Even without starlight above us, I swear his eyes are twinkling.

"They're not real. It's just a glamour. My mother may pretend to be above such things, but she's always been jealous of the mortal sky." *And mortals in general*, I think to myself. There's a reason so many have been enslaved in the castle.

Chapter Nine

Rory

No stars in Faerie? It explains so much… I'd thought it was the constellations that shifted at random, another trick to confound and confuse us mortals…I'd not even considered that they were never there in the first place.

"Another trick," I mutter, the words without heat, and Aries frowns.

"I wouldn't say trick," he says. "Not precisely. I do not believe the glamour was cast out of any ill intent." Which is not to say that my mother wouldn't have been amused if the spell had caused unintended harm.

"No, perhaps not," I agree. For once, I am not in the mood to pick a fight with him. I think, instead, of what I am in the mood for. Some things, like popcorn and salted chips are not possible now — and likely never again. Even if I found another tear, even if I got lucky enough for one to open right at my feet, I am no longer certain I would step through it. I now know how easily the Queen can find me on Earth if she chooses and besides, it's not like life there was much better.

I might not have been a plaything for spoiled faeries, but I'd been at the mercies of every thug and cop who crossed my paths. Beaten for any piece of shine I had on me, conning my way out of arrests with my mouth or ass...no, it hadn't been an improvement.

For better or for worse, Faerie is my home now.

A shitty one, perhaps...but I felt it as soon as I was dragged back through the portal. A sense of belonging I'd never felt anywhere else, like Faerie herself was welcoming me back.

I think it's time that I accept it.

Something inside me clicks into place and with it comes a sense of calm. I roll onto my side, propping my head on my hand. My elbow sinks into the sand. Heat from the fire bathes my back, and Aries looks at me with a question in his eyes.

"Kiss me," I order, my heart *thu-thumping*. I wait, anxious, to see if he will obey. I have not forgotten the role he's played in my past, and I may forever bear the scars, but maybe...maybe I can start to forgive.

Aries doesn't hesitate. Though his eyes widen with obvious surprise, he leans toward me. His hand is gentle as he cradles my face, his other palm as warm as the embers on my back. Then his lips are brushing mine, soft as a feather.

It's not enough. I am not a virgin, needing to be handled like glass. I press in harder, clasping my free hand around the back of his neck and yanking him closer. His teeth dig into my lip by accident but it's as if my blood awakens something inside him.

Aries groans, and then he has me on my back. His mouth is hot on mine. I spread my thighs and he settles immediately between them, pressing his hips into mine. I feel him, hard and hot, against my own throbbing cock.

I break away with a gasp. "You're wearing too many clothes."

"So are you," he growls. He pulls back just long enough to tear off his shirt. I wiggle out of mine as well, then struggle to lift my hips enough to shove my pants down my legs. I get them partway down when he grabs them, dragging them off me. He tosses them, not seeming to care where they end up.

"Yours too," I demand, gripping my dick in a tight fist, watching as he strips down to his skin. I wish it was daylight, if only so I could see every inch of his dark skin clearly. Instead, he is shadow and storm, the firelight glinting on him like lightning.

"Beautiful," I breathe, then he is on me again.

"Tell me to stop and I will," he promises, but he makes no move to penetrate me. Instead, he knocks away my hand and slots our dicks together.

"Fuck!" I curse, my hips lifting on their own to thrust against him. His fingers are hot but soft as velvet as he holds us both.

"Can you come like this?" Aries asks, and he meets my gaze with an intensity I've never seen in him before. "Spill all over my hand and belly? Be my little cumslut?"

I groan and shudder. It's a nasty word, I shouldn't like it…shouldn't want it…but Gods, I do. It's barely been minutes and already I'm throbbing. How long has it been since I've wanted this?

I try to think but my head is foggy with lust. There was a boy back on Earth, a young man with crooked teeth and dark hair, and it had been fun while it lasted.

But it had only lasted a few weeks before we went our own ways. He had found a flat mate and me? I'd found new shadows to run from.

"You're so hard, sweet hart," Aries continues to murmur in my ear.

"I want you to fuck me," I groan, lifting my leg to curl it around his hip and arching my back.

"Not in the sand." Aries twists his wrist instead, an upward stroke that squeezes my dick just right and yet…it's still not enough. I feel hollow, begging to be filled.

"Take me to the water," I demand. Right now, it's hard to believe that there once was a time I'd been terrified to be near so much as a puddle around him.

He goes still, leaning back slightly to meet my gaze. "Is that what you want? Me to take you beneath the waves?"

"Yes," I admit. I am not so fragile now as I was then. He can try to hold me under. My monster will turn him into fish bait. And also…I don't think he will try it. Not here and not now, anyway.

Aries pushes himself to standing. I sit up but before I can do more, he bends down and gathers me into his arms, lifting me as easily as a feather. "Wrap your legs around me," he orders. I do, and he carries me to the water. I feel it tickle the soles of my feet, then wrap around my calves. He walks deeper until it swallows our hips, not stopping until I can feel it lapping gently at my nipples. Aries' hands are strong, one cupping my ass, the other splayed against my back.

He is lovely in the moonlight.

It paints his antlers silver and highlights the lines of his face. His eyes are dark pools. I could drown in them. Aries shifts his right hand from my ass to my thigh, keeping it hitched over his hip as he lowers me down. My other leg stretches out. There are no stones or seashells to poke me, just soft sand. My toes sink in.

Aries, even without his glamour, is taller than me by just enough he has to bend his knees to line us up right. The thick crown of his dick presses against my unprepped hole. Instinctively, I tense, and Aries shushes me. He runs his left hand down my spine and lower, delving beneath my cheeks. His finger is soft as velvet against my entrance and he presses but doesn't enter.

"Please." I breathe the word like a prayer. Suddenly, I need him, more than food or water or air. "Now, please…" Slowly he sinks inside me, his finger long and nowhere near thick enough. I don't know why he's poking at me with them instead of his dick, unless it's a new kink of his. If he insists on using his fingers, though, I want more.

"Another," I order him, though I have no right to demand anything. At best, we are equals here beneath this moon. At worst…well, I am just a Borrowed boy.

He gives me a second finger, and a third when I cry for it, and then he is slotting his dick against me again, still too big for me but no longer so scary. I feel the burn, the stretch, and somehow it is exactly what I need. He sinks into me slowly until our hips are flush, his balls against my ass.

He doesn't move at first, and neither do I. Instead, the cresting waves rock us together. It is a gentle sort of fucking. If I had the courage, I'd go so far as to call it making love. With the soft heat in Aries' eyes, visible even in the darkness of the night…I could even believe it.

Then Aries starts moving, still slow, still graceful, just an inexorable slide out until only his crown rests inside me, stretching my rim. My whimper seems loud in the night.

Again, Aries shushes me, then promises, "I'm not going anywhere now, darling."

Not going anywhere now. I hear the emphasis, but I shove the words away. Instead, I curl my hands around Aries' neck, stretching up until I can claim his lips again. He fucks me slowly and I kiss him like without him, I'll surely die, because for a moment, I believe it.

How am I supposed to walk away from him?

Aries

The Christians speak of their God and their heaven. The Muslims have their Jannah, and Hindus have their Svarga loka.

If I were to believe in an afterlife, I would think I found it here, tonight, buried inside Rory's ass. It's not just the heat of him clamped around my cock, or the way he's so perfectly tight. It's the feel of his lips, soft on mine, and the look in his eyes.

He is looking at me like I mean something to him...maybe even everything. His expression is a mirror to the feelings I have for him that are burning in my chest. The water swirls around us, ebbing and flowing faster the harder I rock into him.

One of his arms curls around the back of my head, his fingers brushing the base of my antlers, and the other tightens around my back as he clings to me. I cling right back — I'd hold him forever if I could.

"I'm...fuck, I'm close," Rory pants, tightening around me.

"Come for me, Rory," I murmur against his mouth. "Spill your seed into the water, let me bathe in it."

And he does, and it is beautiful. Reluctantly, I slip free of him, spilling into the cooling water instead. At least our breath can come together, equally ragged.

Chapter Ten

Marik

"My Queen." Marik prostrates himself against the mossy green carpet in her craft room, his heart thudding in his chest like the hooves of an elk. It's risky, seeking her out, especially here, but he is afraid there is no longer any time left to waste on waiting and fear.

"Did I summon you? I don't believe I summoned you." Queen Nuala pulls her bloody hands free of the pried open ribcage of her latest experiment. A water spryte, Marik guesses, from the iridescent silver skin, but it's hard to be certain. She'd carved away its breasts and ears, lopped off its fingers, and sliced it open from gullet to groin. The poor thing is still alive, if this can be called living, kept alive by the life energy of the troll she'd sewn to it, mouth to mouth.

The troll is held still by catbriers growing into his wrists and ankles. Black, greasy blood has dried on his mottled skin in layers, the freshest still shiny. From where he kneels, Marik can smell his stench, but even that odor is not enough to drown out the stink of shit and rot.

"You did not, my Queen, but I have urgent news that I fear could not wait." Marik drops his eyes quickly, hoping she hadn't seen the disgust he'd felt twisting his face before he wiped it clean again.

"Urgent? I doubt it. Here, come hold this."

Marik looks up. Queen Nuala has her hands in the chest cavity again. Obedient as always, Marik stands up and approaches the table. He takes the still warm, wet organ. There's something wrong with it. It pulses weakly in Marik's hand for a second before failing. Its surface is sticky and coated in what looks like mold.

"That, darling boy, is a spleen. Isn't it beautiful?" Queen Nuala wipes her hands on the spryte's skin. The creature tries to flinch away but succeeds only at tugging on her sutures. Her keening cry is swallowed by the troll.

Queen Nuala just chuckles and steps away from the table. She doesn't bother to close the wound. Marik looks away.

"Come. No, don't set it down," she snaps. He hadn't been planning to, but perhaps she'd seen his fingers clench around it. He nods anyway and follows her to the table and chair in the corner. "There, put it in the bowl." She waves a hand at it. Marik drops the organ inside, wishing he had something with which to wipe the remnants off his skin. He can smell it, putrid with decay, on his fingers.

"My Queen," Marik tries again, "I must speak with you about—"

"Something urgent," she interrupts. "Yes, yes, you said. But I am hungry and I did too much work preparing my breakfast to allow it to grow cold." She picks up the silver blade beside the bowl and stabs it into the spleen. Behind him, the spryte screams as if it can feel it.

Perhaps it can. There's no telling what kind of twisted magic she poured into it during her playtime.

Queen Nuala slices off a piece. She places it on her tongue and savors it like the finest chocolate, closing her eyes as she moans. Her throat moves as she swallows and when she opens her eyes again, they are dark.

She watches him, hungry in more ways than one. "Kneel," she orders. Already anticipating the order, Marik's knees fold immediately. "You look simply ravenous, darling," Queen Nuala purrs. "That simply won't do."

She spreads her thighs and allows him to ruck up the hem of her dressing gown. He knows better than to rush her to the finish. She savors her breakfast, and so does he, ignoring the burn on his lips, the way his tongue blisters. Her thighs clamp tight around his ears and finally, she starts to shudder.

She comes with a cry, but he doesn't stop until she shoves him away. "You've gotten good at that, darling, so good. Aren't you glad I taught you how to put that smart mouth of yours to better use?"

"Yes, my Queen," Marik agrees, the lie like butter on his lips. He stays on his knees, biting into his lip to stop himself from demanding she listen to him now.

She scrapes the last of the bloody organ meat into her mouth, then wipes her lips across the back of her hand. "I'm tired. Take me to bed."

He wants to refuse, and not only because he needs to tell her of the May-tree's death. She's been sleeping longer and longer, and when she dreams...

But he can't refuse.

He takes her to bed.

After, when she's boneless and languid, he kneels again at her bedside. "Now, my Queen? May I share with you my news?" he asks, thinking it safe. Always if he needed something, he's waited until after, and normally, fucked out, she is indulgent.

Today, he realizes, he's misjudged. She smacks him hard, moving so fast he barely sees her move, and his face aches from the pain of it. Immediately, he ducks his head and scuttles backward, debasing himself like a worm until she lies back down and her eyes flutter closed.

Quick and quiet, he departs. As soon as he closes her door behind him, he straightens to his full height. Someone snickers to the side. Some days, he can ignore their humor at his forced servility. The great Marik, the Queen's left hand, bowing and scraping, a joke to those who have never held the Queen's interest.

Today, Marik is already walking the edge of his patience. The snicker, and the disrespect it holds, is enough to shove him over. He alters his path from the stables toward the male fae instead. He is a common wood elf, but clearly one who has risen above his station to be here in the castle. His silks are not as fine as Marik's but far more elaborate than a commoner typically chooses.

His retinue is small, just three other males dressed in similar garb.

"Did someone tell a riddle just before I came out?" Marik demands of him.

The wood elf laughs again, blind to Marik's short temper. "No, my Lord," he answers, his voice oozing arrogance. One of the elf's males, a blond pretty enough to catch Marik's eye and nearly hold it, seems to recognize Marik and sobers. That, or he caught the scent of danger swirling around him—a rabbit in a fox den.

Marik turns his gaze back to the laughing elf. He smiles his best smile. "I don't believe I've seen you at court. What does the wind call you?"

"Sya, of the Eastern Groves." The wood elf gives him a mocking bow.

"Sya, of the Eastern Groves," Marik repeats, his smile sharpening. "The wind calls me Marik. Perhaps you have heard of me."

Now two of Sya's retinue have lost their grins. Sya, though, does not. "I've heard of you, of course. The Queen's bedwarmer. My father said you used to be a mighty warrior."

As if he were not still the most dangerous blade in all of Sidhe lands? As if he was not still the same male who had, single-handedly, bested the legendary Arteria on the battlefield on the Queen's orders. If he were ashamed by anything, it was of taking his former master's life then. The Queen had never meant the captain of her guard to survive the bloody battle against her trolls but she'd underestimated Arteria. He'd emerged from the fight unscathed. He had not survived crossing blades with Marik.

He is not shamed to warm the Queen's bed, not under the shadow of his much larger disgrace.

"And who is your father, Sya of the Eastern Groves?" Marik would like to know who to send the boy's corpse to for planting.

"The wind calls him Oakley. He tends to the largest tree in the woods," Sya boasts. Perhaps it truly is a thing to be proud of, but Marik does not care. Marik's own father, a water aelfe, claims dominion from the mouth of the River of Mirrors all the way to the sea. That had not saved Marik. Why should the status of Sya's sire spare him?

"Don't fret," Marik consoles the not-yet-worried male. "I am sure your father will allow your bones to feed his tree for many years."

Chapter Eleven

Aries

The loch shimmers in the distance. We'd veered toward the Northwest shore in hopes of cutting off some travel time circumventing it. I doubt there will be a boat conveniently waiting for us. I don't know what I was expecting, but a strangely familiar coastline softened by silver sand and water as clear as glass certainly isn't it. It is the loveliest beach I've ever laid eyes on, more so even than the waters of my mother's land.

I stop Rory with an outthrust arm before he can step from the craggy grass. Things here are rarely what they seem, and I do not trust its beauty. Crouching, I brush my fingers through the sand. Nothing happens, so I wait a second before plunging my hand further in.

It is soft and warm and I feel nothing strange.

Rory, surprisingly, waits for me to stand and say it's okay before he steps forward. We both approach the water slowly. Again, he waits for me while I dip my fingers beneath the surface. And again, nothing happens.

I am beginning to suspect that the loch is just a loch.

We refill our water skins, then after a brief discussion, agree to rest here until morning. Neither of us are excited about the thought of climbing the foothills in the dark.

I pitch the tent while Rory pulls one of the bundles of firewood he'd collected in the woods — dry as bone, so it should be easy to burn — out of my bag.

"I hate the water," Rory blurts. He's staring almost pointedly at the fire he's making, as if even the thought of looking at the lake is too much. His shoulders are bunched nearly to his ears.

"Really?" I settle on the soft sand across from him and try to figure out if I knew that. It doesn't make sense. "You used to love the water. How often did I find you on the shores of the Lake of Glass, bathing in the sun?" Too many times, it feels like in my memory. Oh, how he'd taunted me then, flaunting his nudity like a tease.

No, my inner voice scolds me. It is the faerie way of thinking but my time on Earth helped me grow a conscience that I wasn't born with. He'd lain naked on the stones in the sun because I'd not granted him clothing, because I liked looking at him, not because he sought the weight of my eyes upon him.

Whatever teasing I'd read in his body had been manufactured by myself alone.

"That was before," Rory grumbles, his face sullen.

"Before?" I wonder if something happened on Earth. I'd assumed that Rory had stuck to Old York, but I realize immediately that there's no evidence to support that. Just because I'd found him there doesn't mean that was where he started out. And, I realize, just because there was not much water left in the city didn't mean there wasn't enough to have caused him problems. Maybe he'd tried boating.

I'm surprised when Rory glares at me, his eyes nearly black. "Before you drowned me?" He says it like a question but it's obvious that it's not. I'm surprised by his animosity. I wrack my memory, trying to remember a time I'd even come close to drowning him, but nothing.

Rory's eyes narrow further. "You don't even remember?"

"I...don't," I admit, and I'm not sure why. I've never had gaps in my memory before. Then I suddenly remember—not drowning him, but the deal I'd made with the centaur to get back to Faerie. It seems I now know what memory I gave up.

Before I can explain, Rory screams, the sound so filled with pain and anger that I'm frozen in place. He lunges across the fire at me. It surprises me enough that I don't move in time and he takes me to the sand.

For only the second time since our reunion, I see his monster in full.

He is horribly beautiful, just as before. Even as he curls his obsidian claws around my throat and threatens to tear it, I don't move. Instead, I stare. His typically red hair has darkened to the color of old blood but seems to burn, twisting in the windless night around his head like snakes. He is even paler than I realized, now that he is no longer covered in the grave dirt.

Perhaps I would not want to slide my dick between those jaws with their needle-sharp teeth...but with his bottle green eyes, I can't see a monster. I see Rory, different and sharp and lovely.

"Sweet hart," I breathe, the words barely escaping the tight grip he has on me. I don't try to fight him off. Instead, I lift my hand to his face, cradling his cheek. My skin is so dark against his icy translucence. He flinches as if expecting me to strike him but doesn't pull away. "You're lovely."

For a moment, he blinks at me, and I can see as he starts to pull away, feel his claws start to blunt. "No, stay with me," I urge him, overcome by a desire to submit to him like this…submit in a way I've never done for anyone.

I am afraid, but the fear only stokes my arousal higher. Should I be hard like this, with him straddling me, anger flaring in his eyes? I don't know. Rory's hand tightens on my throat, cutting off my breath completely, but only for a second. Then, he lets go, running his nails down my chest instead. They are still sharp, enough that they catch against my shirt and tear, exposing my skin and the long, white lines he leaves behind.

A bit harder and he'd draw blood.

Still, I arch into his touch, not caring when my skin splits open. I wince and his grin only widens.

"Rory was swimming," Rory's monster says, "and it was calm and quiet. Then you showed up, and he was dragged beneath the water."

So. The monster does not consider himself Rory, but something other. On Earth, it happened to humans sometimes, when they'd experienced a trauma too great for their minds to comprehend. A fracturing of the self into multiple personalities. Was this like that? A splintering of his mind? Or is what he calls his monster truly a separate creature, with access to all his memories, all his hopes and fears and dreams?

And does it matter now, in this moment?

I'm not sure.

"Have you ever felt the water close over your face, Princeling?" Rory's monster asks, flattening his hand on my chest and pressing until I can't breathe, until my lungs ache and my ribs start to crackle. "Have you watched the sunlight flicker and fade as you are dragged into the dark? Felt the heat turn to ice and every moment stretch into a thousand years?"

I grip his wrist but don't try to pull him off me, not yet. Rory's hand flexes against me, his nails pricking me again. He must know I can't answer because he continues. "The seaweed dragged him down, dragged him down to the bottom, and everything was quiet, and everything was still. And just as he accepted it and let the peace take him...you yanked him back up."

I don't remember it, but it is exactly the sort of game I would have found funny.

I draw in as much of a breath as I can and fight against his weight to say, "I would not have harmed —" The lie catches in my throat. I hadn't even realized it to be a lie, until it stuck like a stone. I swallow it down, and it burns like a coal in my belly. "I would not have intended true harm," I rephrase.

"And water does not intend to harm the stone, and the fire does not intend to harm the wood." Rory's eyes are green lightning. "Put your hands over your head."

I obey, heart racing.

He leans back slightly, removing just enough of his weight that I can draw in a full, if ragged, breath. He shifts against my hips, seeming to feel my erection against him. "Rory may let you fuck him," his monster snaps, "but I am not Rory. I will not lie placid while you rut into me like a doll for your pleasure. Will *you* spread your legs, Highness?"

"Yes," I gasp, the agreement drawn out of me.

"Show me," Rory's monster orders.

Chapter Twelve

Aries

Embarrassed, I spread my thighs. He can't even see it with how he's straddling me, but I know he can feel it. The humiliation only makes my dick harder, an unexpected knowledge.

"Good little prince," Rory praises sarcastically. With one hand, he grips my jaw, forcing me to meet his eyes. "Should I drag you to the water's edge? Shove your face in the waves while I claim your ass?"

True fear fills me at that. I can survive many things, but even I cannot breathe water. I don't know if he recognizes my terror and backs off, or if he was never truly planning it, but he just grins. "Maybe not. I have no desire to kneel in the mud and slick. Stay. Just like that, pet," he orders, then he stands.

Pet? The nickname chafes something awful...but not enough for me to risk moving. I do not think Rory's monster could truly hurt me, but I don't want to risk him stopping whatever this is, either. I take a chance and turn my head slightly to watch, but nothing more.

Rory digs around in my bag, eventually pulling out a large, plain blanket. He spreads it out on the sand, weighing the corners down with stones. "Now, come here," he orders.

I scramble to my feet, feeling ungainly, and start to walk. Before I can step on the cloth, however, Rory's monster holds up a hand. "Dust off the sand, else this is for nothing. Actually," he adds once I've done so, "why don't you go ahead and strip for me." It was not phrased as a question and I don't take it as one.

I leave my clothes on the sand and only step on the blanket once I am as naked as the day I was blossomed. I go to lie down but Rory stops me with a lifted hand. "Let me look at you, little prince."

Oh, how I hate that nickname...and love it all the same. It stings in just the right way, needling at my ego. Rory's monster circles me like a predator. I flinch as he drags his nail unexpectedly along my spine. "I like you without your glamour," he admits. "Fragile as a flower, you look, but you and I both know the truth. You're tough as an adder, and doubly dangerous."

There are, I suppose, worse things to be compared to.

"Would you kneel for me, if I ask you to?" Rory's monster asks it as if the answer does not truly concern him either way, and yet I suspect that the answer matters more to him now than almost anything. And only that lets me bend my knees.

The sand shifts beneath the blanket, pillow soft.

Rory's monster, still behind me, makes a noise too like a purr to be anything else. He cards his bone-slim fingers through my coils, nails scratching lightly against my scalp. It sends a pleasant shiver through me.

Maybe he realizes it, because he does it again and this time, it drags a quiet moan from my lips. "Ah, I thought you liked that," he says, voice dry. He must bend, because his breath is warm on my ear. "Tell me to stop, and maybe I'll listen."

"I don't want you to stop," I answer. But now I wonder... *If I ask him to, will he? Or will he laugh?*

"Are you sure? If you do..." Rory's monster pauses, his voice momentarily more human when he continues, "just say, 'please, no more', and everything ends. Tell me you understand, Princeling."

"I understand," I reply, throat tight.

"Good boy. Who would have thought my spoiled prince would be so obedient?" Rory's monster circles to the front, towering over me. He is slender, skeletal, but radiating power and strength his size belies.

"Has this been what you wanted this whole time? Someone as strong as you to put you on your knees where you belong?" He looks at me as he speaks with such unadulterated contempt but...somehow, I sense that beneath it is something more. A deep longing and an even deeper satisfaction.

I try to answer but he shushes me with a finger to my lips. "No. For now, the only words I want to hear are your safewords, or silence. Nod if you understand."

And of course, I do.

"I'm going to fuck your pretty mouth, little princeling," Rory's monster tells me, then he strips, tossing his clothes rather carelessly onto the sand. My gaze immediately takes him in.

In some ways, he still looks like Rory — they are the same height, both pale, and both are wiry in frame —

but his fingers are longer and his dick...my heart hammers in my chest at the sight of it.

Rory's cock was a tantalizing mouthful, just big enough to fill my mouth comfortably. Rory's monster's dick is alien. It is long and thick, but more than that, it is ribbed in a way that sends a shudder through me just imagining it rubbing against my prostate.

"Tell me, Princeling...have you taken a dick before?" Rory looks like he knows the answer, and I swallow, shaking my head. I'd hoped he wouldn't ask...hoped I wouldn't need to admit it.

But the shame of it has my own dick as hard as stone. I didn't know that I have a humiliation kink. I'd thought I was too old to learn new things about myself.

"Open up," Rory's monster orders. "No teeth," he adds as I obey. "Stick out your tongue." I do and he rests just the crown of his dick, flushed red, against it. "There you go, just let me..." Slowly, agonizingly slowly, he starts to rock his hips, delving into my mouth a little at a time.

He hits the back of my throat and it's so unexpected, I gag, hands jerking up to grab at his thighs. "Don't touch me," he snaps, swatting my hands away. "Put your hands on your knees and keep them there."

Fuck. The demand pisses me off and I glare at him — but I put my hands on my knees. He smirks down at me with all the arrogance of a young god. He fists my hair again, holding my head still while he ruts into my mouth.

I'm drooling and it's disgusting, degrading...*so why am I so fucking hard?* I want to cover up the evidence but I can't without moving my hands. Instead, I clench them into fists and press them hard against my knees.

"Look at me," Rory's monster demands. My gaze flicks up and I stare at him through watery eyes. The sky behind him has darkened to violet, and his skin looks ethereal in the twilight.

He stops moving, keeping his dick lodged in my throat so deep that I can't breathe, and stares down at me intensely. "I'm going to come in your ass, Aries. You can shake your head if you think it's too dangerous."

Why would it be dangerous, I wonder for a split second, then realize he's referring to my nature as a *leonan sidhe.*

I go still while I think about it and thankfully, he pulls out enough for me to breathe while I do, though he doesn't completely remove himself from my mouth. *Is it dangerous?*

I'm not sure. My mother can drain her lovers by absorbing their seed, but she's a female. In my species, females outnumber the males ten to one. I try to remember the only other male *leonan sidhe* I'd known, Zakariah. But as far as I'm aware, he'd focused his attention on women, so I couldn't be certain.

I shake my head. It's too big of a risk. *I can't lose him.*

Rory's monster lets his dick slide from my mouth and crouches down until we are face to face. He stares at me, his eyes pensive.

"Rory and I are willing to take the risk," the monster finally says, "and it's our risk to take." He looks thoughtful for a moment. "I do not believe your magic can harm us. There is a piece of your magic in here." He takes my hand and presses my palm to the center of his chest. It is hot as the fire that burns on the sand behind him. "A piece of *you* in here. It won't let you harm us."

I can feel it, the thread that binds our souls together, stronger than it's been in years. Is it strong enough?

I sink my teeth into my cock-swollen lips. "You might be right, but...I don't want to watch you fade away like the others. I *can't*."

He grabs my hair with his free hand, tugging my head back. "You *will*, if that's what I want. You're not in control right now, pet."

Fuck. I've always double-fisted the metaphorical leash...I'm not sure I know *how* to let go.

Rory's monster uses my hair to force me onto my back. With his other hand, he yanks my legs, bent uncomfortably beneath me, out and open. I am exposed to the night air, goosebumps raising on my skin despite the flickering campfire.

He settles back on his knees between my thighs.

On my back, his cock looks even bigger. I feel my hole clench in terror. I try to relax, drawing in a deep breath. I almost manage it. But two breaths later, Rory presses against my hole and I clamp down again.

"Wait!" I bark, struggling to close my thighs unsuccessfully.

Rory growls and grabs my legs, holding me still. "Don't fight me." He leans forward, folding me almost in half. His cock nudges me again.

"You can't just shove it in!" I argue, still squirming beneath him. I'd never pictured Rory topping before, but if I had, I wouldn't have guessed him to be an inconsiderate lover.

Rory goes still, frowning down at me. "Why not?" he asks seriously and I realize immediately that he means it truly. He really doesn't know.

"It's not a cunt, it won't stretch on its own. Haven't you..." I try to think how to phrase it. "Am I the only one who's taken you?" I remember back to that night in my cottage, the heat of him clamped around my dick, the way he'd moved like the tide beneath me, his tears like pretty diamonds on his skin.

God, he'd been so fucking tight when I'd slid inside him, the feeling had been unreal.

I freeze, staring into Rory's eyes with horror.

I hadn't prepped him.

Chapter Thirteen

Rory's Monster

"Am I the only one who's taken you?" Aries asks, then immediately looks horrified.

"You don't own us," I snap back, offended. "We can fuck or be fucked by whoever we want." And he has no right to judge Rory, the other half of my soul, for any dick that has entered our body. I'd been right there with him while he took each and every one. We hadn't chosen all of them, but the ones we had chosen were our decision, and ours alone.

The first one on Earth, he'd asked for, spurred on by the stories of the street walkers, just to see how it felt. Rory hadn't hated it, but he'd never felt the pleasure others claimed to feel. Some, he'd taken for money, to pay for his pretty baubles or a bite of food. Then there was Marik, who he took not because he wanted to, but because I'd been sent away, soothed to sleep by what they called *Salvia*.

"I... No, I'm not judging, sweet hart," Aries promises. I don't know if I believe him. Inside me, Rory is listening. He is more conscious now, in this moment, than he's ever been before while I've taken over.

"You say it's not a cunt, that it won't stretch on its own," I tell him, "but with enough effort, we have taken every prick that has sought entry to our body, and all without permanent damage. Is the body of a faerie truly so different?"

Rory is no stranger to pain and through his memories, neither am I. A bit of bleeding, a bit of tearing…it was nothing compared to the Queen's lash or the dancing shoes or any number of other horrors.

Aries, though, goes strangely green. "Let me up," he orders.

With a sigh, I do. I stand and step back into the sand. Aries rolls onto his knees, looking as if he is about to wretch.

I watch him, nonplussed. "If you do not wish to fuck, we do not have to," I finally say to him. "Rory was enjoying the feeling of your mouth just as much."

Inside me, I can practically feel Rory groan.

"Why did you tell him that?" Rory mutters to me.

"Because it is true," I answer him silently. For some reason, I feel as if he is blushing, embarrassed by my words, though I do not understand why he cares that the prince knows of his pleasure.

"You're hopeless," Rory replies.

"Then you deal with him." Petulant, I let myself sink back inside Rory's chest, leaving him to handle the situation. Talking is boring anyway.

Rory

I blink, regaining control of my body as my monster retreats. I can feel him, sullen, beneath my skin. For a second, I feel off-balance, like I've just been woken from a dream. Then Aries groans, dropping his head to his hands, and I concentrate on him.

Frowning, I crouch at the edge of the blanket. "Aries? If you truly are not judging me, then why are you upset?"

He meets my eyes only briefly before his gaze flinches away. "I have wronged you deeply, my love. And I'm only just now realizing it."

"I don't understand," I admit. "The night I spent with you is my most cherished memory, especially now that it isn't tainted by the belief that you abandoned me the morning after." I feel my cheeks heat with embarrassment as I admit to it. I know Aries has had many other lovers, and I know as well that I had been too inexperienced to have been particularly adventurous.

"I don't feel *better* that others have used you as poorly as I have," Aries snaps. I realize quickly that his anger is directed at himself, not me, and try not to react.

"Explain it to me, because I don't understand," I repeat.

Aries speaks slowly, his voice low. "Surely, it must have hurt, taking me like that."

"Of course it did," I answer immediately, still not certain of his point. "It's meant to hurt, it always has. But the pain doesn't mean that I didn't enjoy it. I would gladly hurt a thousand times more to be that close to you again, to feel your chest press so tight against mine that I can feel our hearts beating in time."

"No!" Aries yells, pressing the palms of his hands against his eyes as if to block me from sight. "It's *not* supposed to hurt, not truly, not more than a well-used ache the morning after. I didn't know better then, and I don't deserve to prove it now. I should not have stopped you from entering me, I deserve to feel the hurt I dealt you."

"We were both young then, Aries," I point out. "I'm sure neither one of us knew what we were doing." I knew that he'd lain with dozens of fae before me, but they were a hardy breed, much more so than a human, and most of them could heal themselves with little more than a thought, unless the wound was made by salt or iron. I could hardly expect the mechanics to be the same.

Aries refuses to uncover his eyes.

Thinking fast, I try a different tactic. "Show me now."

"Show you what?" Aries asks, his voice strained.

"Show me how it *should* feel. I have the right to know, don't I?" I lift my brow. If he doesn't touch me now, I fear he will never touch me again. I'm not sure I could bear it — our time together is so limited already. I can't imagine sex without pain, but if ever I'm going to experience it, I want it to be with him.

Aries looks at me with his heart in his eyes. "I can't bear the thought of hurting you again, Rory. I would rather cut off my own hands than let them harm you."

"Then don't hurt me." Slowly, I kneel in front of him. "Teach me, Aries."

He is a man torn in two. I can see his indecision on his face even in the darkness that surrounds us. The only question left is not whether he will break, but how.

"I do not deserve to look upon you, let alone lay a finger upon your form," Aries finally says, slipping close to the archaic language of our youth, "but I will do as you say."

"I don't want a pity fuck, Princeling," I reply, purposefully crude. "I want you to fuck me, and I want you to like it."

Aries finally relaxes a little, though tension still sits around his eyes. "How could I do anything else?"

Now that he's on board, I suddenly feel nervous. Not about the sex, not truly...but there's an intensity in his eyes as he stares at me. "Lie down for me, sweet hart. On the blanket," he adds, stopping me from dropping back onto the sand. I obediently shift forward to where he gestured.

Above me, the sky is dark and starless. For a moment, it distracts me, the empty black nothing above us, but then Aries crawls toward me. Gently, he nudges open my thighs.

He slides his fingers over my knees, then trails them, soft as feathers, over my inner thighs. The shudder that wracks my body is like nothing I've felt before already, and he's barely touched me.

"First," Aries says, "start with a tease. Find all the spots that make your partner — yes, like that," he interrupts himself as his fingers skim up my sides and my back arches on its own. "Feel it?"

"It...oh!" I cry out as he rubs the thumb of his right hand over my left nipple, so gently that if my eyes were closed, I might have imagined it to be the wind. "Again!" I demand, and he complies, then takes the thumb of his left hand to my right nipple as well.

I've had them pinched and bitten. They've been flogged and clamped, even pierced, though the holes have scarred over. I'd come to believe that they were numb to feeling anything...but apparently, they had only grown numb to pain. His feather-light touches are an agony all of their own.

He doesn't stop toying with them until they are hard as diamonds and flushed red. Only then does he remove his hands. I sag in relief, until he bends forward and takes one in his mouth.

"Oh fuck!" I curse, grasping at his head, though I don't know if I want to hold him closer or shove him away. Then he starts to suck and somehow, the feeling gets even better.

Aries switches between each of my nipples until even the ghost of his breath against them is enough to have me quivering, then finally relents. He settles over me until his face is hovering over mine. I wish it was lighter so I could see him better.

"Lovely," Aries murmurs, staring into my eyes like he's waiting for the answer to a question he hasn't asked. He slides one hand between us, skimming it down my chest and over my cock before he dips between my thighs. He rubs the tip of just one finger against my ass and I can't help but to tense.

"Relax," Aries whispers. "Breathe with me and push out—yes, like that, I've got you." Slowly, he pushes just the tip of his finger into my hole and I'm surprised that it doesn't hurt. "Just take the one for now, let me touch you..."

And I do, and it's nearly perfect. He moves slowly, careful not to move too fast or too hard, and soon enough I'm a mewling mess beneath him. "Another!" I finally demand, and fire flares in Aries' eyes.

He pulls his finger free but when he doesn't immediately replace it, I growl up at him.

"Patience, Rory," Aries teases. "I'm not taking you dry."

I don't know what he means but it doesn't take long to figure it out. I watch him slip his hand between us again and cradle the crown of his leaking dick in his palm, gathering up the slick, slippery pre-cum leaking from it like a sieve. When he returns his fingers — two this time — to my ass, they are wet and enter me smoothly.

Now, there is a sting, but it's so miniscule compared to what I'm used to that I hardly notice. My hips arch seemingly on their own as my ass tries to swallow him down to the knuckles. "Come on, Princeling, fuck me like you — fuck!" I curse and break off my words as he drags his fingertips over my magic button, sending lightning coursing through my body. "There!"

"Don't worry," Aries chuckles, "I know what I'm looking for." He proves it by prodding at it again and I can't hold back my shout. It echoes across the water. "I'm going to add a third now," Aries promises and for a second, I want to hit him. He sounds too calm considering how he's taking me apart like this.

Then he adds a third — and eventually a fourth — and I can't think of anything at all.

And the only thing I feel when he slides his dick into me is an orgasm so intense, for a second I imagine I see stars.

Chapter Fourteen

Marik

The pretty young wood elf does not die slowly. Not because he is a good fighter — he's clearly never thrown a punch before, let alone taken one — but because Marik needs an outlet for his anger, and for this feeling he can't even name... Like failure, but more. He'd tried to warn the Queen. She hadn't listened, and now...what terror would creep into their borders without the May-tree to shield them? Already, the Queen's nightmares are leaving their mark on the Kingdom. How much worse would things get?

So he does not kill Sya quickly, does not grant him the mercy of an easy death. This, he would not fail at. He takes the wood elf apart piece by piece, until the tiles are slick with syrup-sticky blood and the whole castle echoes with the song of his screams.

Only then, when Sya's lungs no longer rattle with breath, does Marik drag the boy's body to the barracks.

He barks an order at the first of his men that he sees. "Deliver this to the Eastern Groves, to an elf named Oakley. Tell him to better guard the tongues of his other spawn if he does not wish to see them planted as well."

"Yes, sir!" Asahi snaps off a salute then relieves him of his burden. Marik does not bother wiping off his hands before he returns to the castle, detouring to the kitchen. He snags the arm of a passing brownie, leaving a smear of blood on her dark skin. She cringes but does not wipe it away.

"Send water to my rooms for a bath," he orders her.

She sketches a wobbly curtsey and babbles out, "Of course, my Lord!"

He watches her scuttle away before he turns his glare on the cook, the kobold named Penny. "Send up a tray, as well."

Penny bites her lip, looking distressed as she nods.

He knows that she will hear his unspoken request—that she send it up along with a boy he can take his mood—not sated with the wood elf's death—out on. Not all of the Borrowed ones are free to play with. Ever since the Queen made that treaty with the mortals on the other side of the veil, they've grown fewer and fewer in number. There is no more snatching of babies from their cradles or luring children away from wooded paths and concrete playgrounds.

Oh, how the Queen had raged over that, the loss of her perfect slaves. For days he'd labored under her anger until he'd broken, blurting out a solution he now regrets.

No females are permitted in the palace, that is the law…but the law has never applied to the humans they Borrowed. The human women pop out babies with a terrifying rapidity. The process is bloody and often messy, he'd quickly realized, nothing like the elegant blossoming of his kind, but they flourish like a cancer.

Unfortunately, the human children age slowly in Faerie. It would be centuries, as they count time on the mortal side of the veil, before any of them are old enough for him to do more than tease. It means he and the other fae need to be more careful with the grown ones until then. Worse, it also means no more killing them, either.

Every Borrowed female was sent to the breeding pits and every male is rotated through mating seasons. To own a Borrowed one now is to accept that they belong ultimately to the Queen and to accept their absence for at least one sennight every month.

Now, fewer and fewer fae are willing to share their pets.

Marik leaves the cook to her work, knowing she won't dare disappoint him, and heads up to his room. His bath is waiting, steaming hot. He soaks in the water until he is as clean as a seal, emerging only when a tentative knock sounds on the door.

He climbs from the tub and doesn't bother to dry himself. He snags a silk robe and drapes it carelessly over his shoulders. He leaves it untied as he crosses the floor and yanks open the door. The Borrowed man is older than Marik prefers, his eyes and hands showing the lines of his age, but Marik cannot afford to be picky.

"Come in," Marik orders, and the man obeys.

Before Marik can send him to his knees, though, he hears it—a terrible screaming from the Queen's bedchamber. He barely has time to brace himself against his door before the floor beneath him starts to shake. At first it rolls like the deck of a ship at sea, then it grows stronger. He is knocked to his knees and the sound of the earth roaring fills his ears. A mirror slips from his wall, crashing to the stone floor and shattering.

Just as he starts to fear — truly fear — that the castle is going to come down around him, the shaking stops. Heart pounding, he waits. A second, smaller quake, then a third, and it is over.

It is not the first quake he has felt since the Queen's nightmares started, but it is the strongest. From the hallway, he can hear other faeries start to laugh. Most of the court is too hooked on wine and herbs to understand the danger they are in. The Borrowed man in front of him, though…his eyes are wide with terror, his skin ashen.

Marik glares at the shattered glass in the corner of his room. In one of the larger shards, he can see his reflection. It is glaring at him, accusing.

"Go," Marik orders the Borrowed man, no longer in the mood to play.

A devoted lover would go check on the Queen, as would a loyal servant. Instead, he leaves his room to go check on the horses. He knows few others will think to do so. Ahead of him, the Borrowed man flees quickly down the stairs, as if worried Marik will change his mind.

Marik knows this is his fault, all of it. For not being able to convince the Queen to listen…for not killing the Queen when he had the chance. And he has had every chance — who else is permitted to sleep at the foot of her bed? Who else has entered her body as many times as he?

You carry the guilt for more than that, a snide little voice scolds him. *It's your fault the prince fled…your fault he's not here to challenge his mother for the throne.*

Your fault.
Your fault.
Your fault.

Chapter Fifteen

Aries

The loch shimmers in the distance. We'd veered toward the Northwest shore in hopes of cutting off some travel time circumventing it. I doubt there will be a boat conveniently waiting for us.

You know that there won't be, a small, familiar voice whispers, gone before I can register it.

I don't know what I was expecting, but a too-familiar coastline softened by silver sand and water as clear as glass certainly isn't it. It is the loveliest beach I've ever laid eyes on, more so even than the waters of my mother's land.

I stop Rory with an outthrust arm before he can step from the craggy grass. Things here are rarely what they seem, and I do not trust its beauty. Crouching, I brush my fingers through the sand. Nothing happens, so I wait a second before plunging my hand further in.

It is soft and warm and I feel nothing strange.

You've touched these grains of sand before... the little voice whispers, fuzzy in my ears. I shake it clear. It's not possible. This is the farthest I've traveled from the Sidhe lands. When would I have had the chance?

Rory, surprisingly, waits for me to stand and say it's okay before he steps forward. We both approach the water slowly. Again, he waits for me while I dip my fingers beneath the surface. And again, nothing happens.

I am beginning to suspect that the loch is just a loch.

We refill our water skins, then after a brief discussion, agree to rest here until morning. Neither of us are excited about the thought of climbing the foothills in the dark.

I pitch the tent while Rory pulls one of the bundles of firewood he'd collected in the woods — dry as bone, so it should be easy to burn — out of my bag.

Swallowing, I stare at the shimmering water, then turn to Rory. "Does something about this seem...familiar?"

"Hm-mm?" Rory looks up from the fire he's started to stare out at the water. His teeth dig into his lip. "You know, now that you mention it, I feel like I had a dream about somewhere like this. We were..." His skin goes pink and I know exactly what we were doing in his dream.

For some reason, I feel like I've had the same one. I can picture us standing together, waist deep in the loch, rocking together until our seed spills out into the water, and I can picture us sprawled, limbs entangled, on a blanket in the sand.

Something sharp stabs behind my eyes and I grimace, slamming them shut and pressing my fingers against them.

"Aries?" Rory's voice is quiet and a little worried. "Is something wrong?"

"Just a headache," I reply, rubbing my fingers up over my forehead.

"Probably dehydrated," Rory says. "Here. We can refill it again before we leave, no point in being precious with it now." He holds out one of the water skins and I take it, obediently swallowing a few mouthfuls of water. Slowly, the headache seems to recede. Not all the way, but enough that I can think again.

"Better?" Rory asks, and I nod.

The fire crackles between us, then Rory says, "You think there's any fish in this water?"

* * * *

The loch shimmers in the distance. We'd veered toward the Northwest shore in hopes of cutting off some travel time circumventing it.

Aries, you need to wake up. You've lost so much time.

I doubt there will be a boat conveniently waiting for us.

I don't know what I was expecting, but a coastline softened by silver sand and water as clear as glass certainly isn't it. It is the loveliest beach I've ever laid eyes on, more so even than the waters of my mother's land.

Wake up, Aries… Open your eyes.

I stop Rory with an outthrust arm before he can step from the craggy grass. Things here are rarely what they seem, and I do not trust its beauty.

For a split second, I see bones in the sand, but then I blink and the beach is empty. I shake my head to clear it and step forward.

Crouching, I brush my fingers through the sand. Nothing happens, so I wait a second before plunging my hand further in.

It is soft and warm and I feel nothing strange.

Look around, Aries. Look around and remember!

I blink at the silver grains of sparkling silt as I pull my hand free. Sand slips through my fingers. Blinking, I look around. *Remember?* Remember what?

Then, I do. I remember catching rainbow oarfish, and the look on Rory's face as he feasted on their tender flesh. I remember taking him in the lake, the warm water cradling us, and taking him on the sand, teaching him to know pleasure. And I remember fighting, him screaming that he hated me as he shoved me beneath the water.

I remember living this day a dozen times over at least. Standing abruptly, I step back onto the grass. "We need to keep moving," I tell Rory, my voice strained. "It's not safe."

"How do you know?" he asks. He stares toward the water and I can see the longing in the green depths of his eyes.

"Because I remember," I answer.

"Shouldn't we...?" Rory lifts the water skin and shakes it. The sound is hollow. He gestures with it to the water.

"Definitely not. We need to keep moving." I hate to say it. We're both dehydrated and I don't know how long it will take us to find another source of water, but at least I know that no matter how thirsty we get, dehydration won't kill us. Make us miserable and weak, maybe...but we won't die.

I can't say the same if we stay here.

Rory's face drops, then he sets his jaw. "Well, I'm not moving. I like it here. It feels…quiet. And I'm thirsty. If you want to keep moving, then do it, but I'm staying here." He turns his back on me and starts to walk — though stomping would be more accurate, as much as one can stomp through shifting sand — toward the lake.

Heat boils beneath my skin. Anger, at first — *how dare he walk away from me?* — but it quickly morphs to panic. "Rory!" I call as I follow him, desperate to stop him from touching the water. I don't know for sure what's kept us stuck here — if it's the sand, we're already too late — but everything inside me is screaming that the problem is in the loch itself. The water was too peaceful to be anything but a threat.

"Shut up! You're not my boss!" Rory screams back, and it's so irrational that I freeze for a second. My hesitation is enough to get him two steps closer to the shore. I burst into action, my long legs covering the distance between us in two bounds. I catch him just before the sand turns to mud and tackle him to the ground.

He struggles beneath me. His eyelids tense as he opens his eyes wide, his eyebrows pulled together above them. I recognize the emotion. I've seen it on his face too often.

Terror. It breaks something inside me.

That fear is of *me.* I see it, recognize it, and yet, can do nothing. I cannot let him touch the loch. Even if he hates me for it, even if it means knocking him out and carrying him away, I will not let Faerie snare him again.

Rory bucks violently beneath me and I settle my weight on his hips, keeping him from rolling free. He strikes me with his hands, forcing me to snare his wrists and pin them, and the whole time, I'm talking to him, trying to get through to him.

He's beyond listening, and I feel it when he slips away. His body goes still as a statue, every muscle corded like steel. His gold-flecked green eyes turn to jade fire, bottle green and bright as the color washes from his skin and his mouth fills with daggers. Droplets of violet blood dot his lips.

"Princeling," Rory's monster growls at me. His emerald flame eyes are flashing. "Let us up."

I loosen my hands but don't release him. Strange though it may be, I sense that Rory's monster — *I need to find something else to call him* — will listen to me better than Rory would.

"I can't," I tell him. "Not until you promise to listen."

"Let me up, and I promise to consider it." He narrows his eyes. "Don't, and we will see how well you can speak without a throat." He bares his needle-sharp teeth.

Slowly, terrified he's going to continue his flight to the water as soon as I do, I uncurl my hands from around his wrists and sit back, though I don't climb off him fully. "The water is dangerous. We need to leave, and quickly, before it snares us again. This is not the first time we've lived this day. Do you understand?"

Rory's monster doesn't answer right away. Instead, he goes quiet, his eyes distant, and I suspect he is talking to Rory. He confirms it when he answers, "It's too late. The water already has him."

"Fuck!" I curse, glaring up at the sky.

"Don't worry. I believe its hold on him will lessen the farther we get from here," he reassures me, and when I meet his eyes, they are strangely soft.

"How do you know this?" I ask, genuinely curious. I want to understand him. He is a part of Rory, which makes him a part of this. Whatever *this* is.

"I don't know…" His eyebrows twitch lower and he presses his lips together for a second, then shrugs a shoulder. "I just do. We should leave soon. The longer we stay here, the stronger the pull to the water is growing. I can ignore it for a while, but Rory will take over eventually. He's not happy with either of us right now."

"You're right. Will you…" I pause, gathering my thoughts as I push myself to my feet, hoping I can trust him not to run as soon as he's free. "Can you tell him I'm sorry for frightening him?" It's a trivial thing to care about now, I know, but I never want to see that expression on his face again.

"He can hear you. He just doesn't care." He pushes himself to his feet and starts strolling back up the beach, away from the water. "Come on. Didn't you say there's no time to waste?"

I follow, amused at the way he's taken charge. Hurrying up to his side, I ask the question I've been meaning to ask for a while now. "What should I call you?"

"Whatever you want, I suppose," he answers, his voice dry. "I doubt I can stop you from calling me anything."

"No, I mean…what do you *want* me to call you?" I clarify, realizing that he seems to take things more literally than I intend.

"Why would I care? I am who I am, no matter what you decide to call me." He looks at me and this time, I see the humor dancing in his eyes. They catch the sunlight and twinkle.

He's teasing me. I grin back. "So I can keep calling you Rory's little monster and you wouldn't mind?"

He laughs. "Why would I? Rory calls me that all the time."

I tap my chin like I'm seriously thinking, then muse, "Maybe I should call you Earl? Or Donald?" Both old-fashioned names have long since fallen out of fashion. Neither would do him justice.

"No!" he practically shouts, his face quite a picture. A mix of horror and amusement, and beneath it all, what seems like wistfulness. I suspect he likes the idea of having a name of his own more than he is letting on.

"So, you *do* care what I call you. Good to know."

We've finally left the sand behind. Beneath our feet, the grass is short and wilted. Rounding the lake from back here will take longer, and I know that the whole time we walk, the water will be right there, to our right, beckoning us to come closer for a drink, but already I can feel its pull lessening on me. I can only hope it's doing the same for Rory and his monster.

"Angel," I blurt as soon as it comes to me. "I'm going to call you Angel."

He looks horrified. "Angel? Do I *look* like a fat, white-winged, halo-wearing choir boy?"

"No, but you're here to keep Rory safe, aren't you? You protect him when he gets scared or if he's in danger...just like a guardian angel." The more I think through it, the more perfect I find it.

"It's...I mean...yes, I suppose I do but...really? Angel?" The look he sends me is plaintive. I can't help but find it—and him—adorable.

"Unless you have a better idea, then yes. Really."

He purses his lips, then sighs. "Whatever. Call me Angel if it makes you happy."

"You know, I think it does." I bump his shoulder with mine and laugh.

Chapter Sixteen

Angel

Rory's princeling confuses me. He is a walking contradiction. In Rory's memories, the faerie is tall and broad of shoulder, with a cocky grin and cold eyes. But Rory also remembers his soft hands and, always, that one single night of joy before it all fell apart. Now, walking beside me on the sand, he is slender, narrow of waist and trim as a swimmer, and his eyes twinkle with laughter.

"Bastard. Stupid faerie prince with his...stupid face!" Rory snarls inside our body. His anger burns hot like coals. I feel it as if through a pane of glass, one layer removed.

"You are being irrational," I scold him.

"Irrational? Irrational?" he screeches like a fishwife, and I wince, rubbing at our ears even though his voice is really coming from in my mind. Knowing that and feeling it are two different things.

"I won't talk to you like this. Why don't you take a nap?"

"What am I, a toddler?" He grumbles at me, pouting like the child he claims he isn't. He doesn't stop whining but I do my best to block him out.

Instead of listening, I turn to stare at his princeling again, examining his profile as I try to see what it is about him that holds such sway over Rory. He's attractive enough, but no more so than many of the men Rory had lain eyes on back on the streets of Old York. Though I do admit the coils that have formed since his hair has started growing out are…distracting.

"What?" Aries asks, meeting my eyes. "Is there something on my face?"

"Just the usual things. A nose, a mouth…two eyes," I reply, not dropping my gaze. "I'm trying to figure out what Rory sees in you."

"Should I be insulted?" Aries asks, lifting an eyebrow in question.

"Do you consider his attention insulting?" I counter, lifting my own eyebrow.

"Of course not. Why would I? But *you* clearly don't find me worthy of it," Aries answers.

"I did not say you were not worthy of it. I said I was trying to understand. His feelings for you are… complicated." I say, weighing my words.

"What are you doing?" Rory snaps out of his whining to ask.

I ignore him as I try to explain, "He likes the way your face is put together, but looking at your face brings up bad memories."

"Stop! Don't tell him anything!"

Aries grimaces. "I've apologized for that."

"I know. And he believes you. Most of the time, he even accepts it," I say. "But putting a bandage on a wound doesn't make it go away. Do you remember the mural in that alley?" Perhaps it seems a strange segue — Aries certainly looks confused as he nods. "Did you sense the magic in it? The spell he wove into the paints with his own blood and sweat?"

Aries frowns, clearly struggling to remember, but he shakes his head again. "If there was magic in it, I was too injured to notice at the time."

"He spent years searching for the right set of spells. As soon as he found it, he painted away his most painful memory, trapped it in the paint on that wall until your blood broke the seal. Do you know what he locked away?

Inside me, Rory is silent as a grave.

Aries presses his lips tightly together as he shakes his head, visibly uncomfortable.

"It wasn't the uncountable years of suffering at your mother's hands, or your friends'. It wasn't even the day you almost drowned him. His most painful memory is the night he spent in your bed. He's tried to explain it to me but I don't understand. How could a night that caused him minimal physical pain hurt worse than being tortured?" I am truly curious.

I'm even more curious when I see the agony cross Aries' face. I didn't lay a finger on him and yet, my words have hurt him. Why?

"You have the emotional range of a paper plate," Rory snaps at me. I feel him fight to surface, to take the reins back over his body, but I can still feel the water to our right trying to snag him. It's not safe yet. I shove him down.

"There is more than one kind of pain," Aries answers me weakly. He walks faster, like he's hoping to outrun me…or whatever demons my words have stirred.

"I want to keep him safe. How can I protect him from something I cannot see? Something I don't understand?" I press, hurrying to keep up with him. "He aches inside, but I cannot take his memories from him. And…I don't think he would let me if I could."

"Sometimes, no matter how much we want to, we can't protect the ones we love from everything. I would wrap him up in cotton and hide him away from the world if I thought he would let me," Aries says.

"It's going to hurt him when you leave," I say with a sigh. "How do I protect him from *that*?"

Aries, unfortunately, does not have an answer for me.

We walk together in silence.

"*I hate you,*" Rory whines in my head.

"*No you don't.*"

Two days later, I'm beginning to think that I hate *him* for making me do this.

No sleep, minimal breaks…it feels like torture. Unfortunately, that's just how long it takes us to round the loch and follow the river that feeds into it through the foothills of the mountains. I've never been at the wheel, so to speak, of Rory's body for this long.

Rory stopped grumbling by dusk the night before. Mostly, I suspect, because with me at the helm, he doesn't have to feel the aching in his thighs or the burning of his eyes from lack of sleep. It's a different kind of pain than I'm used to.

Now, I stare at the path through the mountains that Aries is adamant we use and feel like crying. "You have to be joking. You're joking, right? You can't seriously expect me to make it up that?" I gesture toward the pass. It's steep and craggy, barely more than an animal path. Rory's body isn't even wearing shoes. Does he think I can't see the snow at the mountain peaks?

"*You wanted to be in control,*" Rory mocks me.

"There are no other options. If that map is accurate, there's no way around. We can go over, or we can go back," Aries answers.

"We can't go back…" I hate to admit it, but it's true. Going back would be a death sentence. I look left and right but unfortunately, I don't see an easier looking path.

"It will be dark soon and we can find a place to camp then," Aries promises.

"Why don't you come out now?" I ask Rory, trying not to sound like I'm begging. By now, our memories of the many days and nights at the loch have returned and he's no longer begging to go back. Surely it's safe enough for him to take over.

He just laughs.

None of us are laughing by the time we stumble on a good enough place to camp. It has been dark for what feels like ages but the ground was sloping so steadily that there was no good place to stop. Setting up camp on the incline would not only be uncomfortable but dangerous. We'd be taking the risk of rolling back down the mountain. And it's not even like we can pretend we are making good progress. Despite it feeling like we've been walking forever, when I look at the path we have ahead of us, it feels like we haven't climbed at all.

Finally, we stumble on a spot where the path levels out and two boulders have fallen together just right, leaving a clear patch of ground beneath them that would be perfect for building a fire. It would be shielded from the wind and, hopefully, the stones would hold enough heat to radiate warmth all night long. Already, the air around us is chilly enough to bite.

Aries rolls out our bedrolls while I stare at the dry wood I've gathered and carefully arranged into a little teepee. I strike the flint against the flat stone again, sending sparks cascading onto the kindling, but they fizzle and die almost immediately.

Rory makes building fires look easy.

I try again with no success, my failure pulling a growl from my throat.

"Oh, don't get your panties in a twist, I'll do it!" Rory finally says and, grateful, I let him swim to the surface.

"Thank the gods…"

Rory

My monster—who Aries has apparently renamed Angel of all things—flees back inside me like all the hounds of hell are on his heels. I've seen him face down mobsters and muggers but apparently, building a small fire is where he draws the line.

I blink my eyes as I struggle to get used to being back in my body again, swaying slightly as I acclimate. For a second, I feel the urge to turn around and head back to the loch but the feeling is faint and quickly fades away. I shake my head, embarrassed at how easily the water had snared me and I hadn't even noticed.

Aries must think me so weak.

Angry at myself, I kneel beside the wood and rearrange it for better airflow, then strike the flint hard on the stone, aiming the sparks at the pile of dry kindling Angel had gathered. It was a good first effort from a creature who had never needed to make fire before. If he hadn't started getting so frustrated, I do believe he would have figured it out eventually.

Slowly, it crackles to life. I watch it closely, poking at the embers until I'm certain it won't go out, then retreat to my bedroll. Aries looks at me, then does a double take. "Rory? You're back?"

"Angel was getting tired of walking," I explain. Aries looks...embarrassed? I smirk. "Oh, did you think I wasn't listening to you both?"

"I mean...he said you were but..."

"But what? He did tell you he couldn't lie," I say with a laugh.

"Lots of people say they can't lie. That doesn't mean they're telling the truth. You know how many half-fae try that on during interrogations? You learn really quick that just because someone looks fae, or claims to be held by the Sooth, doesn't mean they actually are," Aries explains.

"Well, I suppose that means you won't believe me either, but he really can't lie." My words are muffled at the end by a yawn I can't fight down.

Aries takes pity on me. "I'll take first watch. Why don't you get some sleep?"

Normally, I would argue but not today. Angel may have had control of my body but that doesn't mean I hadn't been awake the whole time. Watching him move my body around was almost more exhausting than doing it myself. It's like some part of me is fighting against him the whole time. He's promised me that it feels different to him, that when I'm at the helm, he is hibernating, as he calls it.

I crawl into my bedroll and tug the fabric over my face to block the light of the fire, falling asleep almost immediately.

Chapter Seventeen

Marik

The other faeries are holding a revel in the ballroom as if the castle had not threatened to fall moments ago. Marik stares at them in disgust as he passes by on the way to the stables.

If only the Queen hadn't loosened the restrictions on faerie wine. The old queen had banned its use during her reign. In her many writings, she'd written of its dangers — turning faeries into little more than shells seeking the next party, the next hit. Her prohibition had lasted well into Queen Nuala's rule.

Marik doesn't know what changed, but some time before he was Blossomed, the Queen had reintroduced it to the Court. He'd experimented with it — they all had, even the prince — but Marik never liked how it made him feel. Like nothing mattered but the next drink. The four of them — he and the prince, and Alberich and Anwynn — had vowed never to partake of it again.

Marik pulls his eyes from the revel and leaves the castle behind. He doesn't want to see what has become of his former friends. Anwynn and Alberich — now Wren and August — had kept their promise for a while after the prince left, but they'd fallen to the wine eventually. First August, then Wren shortly after.

He didn't see them in the ballroom today, but he assumes they are in there somewhere.

They always are.

He is nearly to the stables when he feels it — the ground shaking beneath his feet again. Never have the shakes come this close together before. He freezes where he stands, listening.

Faerie doesn't talk to him, not like she does to Aries, but he can sense enough of her feelings to tell she's angry. More than angry…terrified.

He turns to stare at the castle. For a moment, everything seems calm.

Just as he starts to wonder if it is just another aftershock, the ground starts to rumble again. The castle *ripples*, just like a reflection in a stone-skipped lake. The first stone falls, then another, and then it is a rockslide of tumbling walls and shattered glass.

From inside, he hears the screaming.

Marik doesn't rush for the castle to try to evacuate his fellow courtiers. Instead, he hurries into the stables, flinging open doors and freeing the trapped horses in hopes of sparing their lives when the ceiling inevitably comes down.

Orchid pauses beside Marik for just long enough to brush her pale head against his shoulder in thanks before she flees. He doesn't have time to watch her. He turns to the last stall and releases Aphid. The stall door is still swinging open when the ground gives the largest quake yet and the ceiling starts to fall around him.

* * * *

Aries

The path up the mountain is steep and narrow. More than once, I stumble, nearly sliding back down, and Rory is having a worse time than I. I'd given him his cloak back, but that only helps so much when he doesn't have shoes. He claims that his bare feet make it easier for him to grip the roots and stones that form the trail, but I can see the way he winces the farther we climb, especially as the air grows colder.

I don't know how to help him. I can't give him my boots—even if I can convince their magic to allow it, they would be far too big, and besides being painful, there's too much of a risk that blisters could get infected. I'd sacrifice another shirt—not that we have many left—but it would likely freeze to his skin and do more damage than leaving them bare would.

I wish I'd packed my bag with a second person in mind. Or even a prolonged journey. We'd long since eaten all the travel food, and though we'd been lucky enough to find some berry patches on the climb, the small handfuls of berries we'd scavenged wouldn't keep our bellies full for long.

Guilt twists at me as Rory stumbles again, slamming into my side and nearly falling before I can catch him. "Okay, that's enough," I finally break. "It's too cold for you to keep walking without shoes. Climb on my back, I'll carry you."

Rory looks up at me, his expression tense. It's obvious to me that he's thinking, and thinking hard. "I want to argue," he finally says, "but I'm not *that* stubborn." It doesn't take him long to scramble up onto my back and lock his arms around my neck and ankles around my waist. I find myself more grateful than ever for his small frame.

Normally, I would hardly notice the extra weight— I've carried backpacks heavier than him. As steep as the pass is getting, though, I know I can't afford a single misstep.

By the time the sky grows dark above us, my fingers are freezing and my palms shredded from using the roots and stones to pull myself up the near vertical path. I can hear Rory's teeth chattering in my ear.

"Keep an eye out for a safe place to stop," I ask Rory, then grunt as I drag us another few feet up the trail.

Silently, I ask Faerie for aid. Her response is quiet. *Keep going. You'll see it soon.*

And soon, we do. A cave, just off the path. The opening is narrow and I nearly miss it in the dark, but then Rory jerks against me, clutching me tight with one hand while he points with the other. "There!"

I whisper my gratitude to Faerie and slowly angle myself toward the opening. Just off the path, it's even more difficult to climb, but thankfully we don't have to go far. I drag us into the cave and look around carefully before I allow Rory to slide down.

It's cold, but not as cold as it was out in the bitter wind, and it's dark, but a fire will fix that. "Stay here," I say, urging Rory toward the stone just inside the opening. "Let me look around."

He huffs but doesn't argue, a tiny miracle. I pace around the cave. It curves around at the back but ends in a solid wall. The only way in or out is the way we came. At least no one can sneak up on us.

"Can I build a fire now?" Rory asks as soon as I come back to him. "It's freezing." He's rubbing his palms up and down his arms, and shifting his weight from foot to foot on the stones.

"Yes, of course. Let me help," I answer, frowning at the center of the cave where a ring of stones and the remnants of an old fire already wait. It is cold, but the fact that it is here at all concerns me. Someone had climbed the same path we were on now, and recently enough that the ashes from their fire haven't blown away. Were they climbing up or down? More importantly, were they friend or foe?

I reach into my bag to pull out the firewood — but there is nothing left.

I drop to my knees and put the bag on the ground in front of me, as if I'll have better luck from a different angle. "We must have used the last of the firewood."

Rory's cheeks go pale. "How long were we caught by the loch?"

I wish I had an answer for him but I just shake my head. I can't be certain. Ten days, maybe, give or take. However long it had been, it was enough for us to burn through most of our supplies.

"Stay here," I suggest. "Maybe there's something we can use outside…"

"There wasn't," Rory answers. "The path has been mostly rock for hours. It'll take too long for you to reach the trees again, and even if you do and manage to make it down, by the time you get back up here, it'll be nearly morning."

I know he's right. The path had been growing steeper for quite some time. Descending in the dark would be too dangerous to risk.

"Fuck!" I curse, angry at myself for not thinking to check our supplies before we started our ascent, and for letting the loch snare us in the first place.

"Honestly, it's not even that cold," Rory says, clearly trying to calm me down. "I've slept in worse back in Old York and it didn't kill me."

"Is that supposed to make me feel good?" I snarl at him, spinning on my heels and facing away so I don't have to stare at the expression on his face. I shouldn't be yelling at him. It's not his fault—*none* of this is his fault.

"I'm sorry," I force myself to apologize. "I wish I had the softest sheets to lay you down on, and a hearth to keep you warm."

"And I wish you weren't going to leave me at the end of this journey," Rory says, his voice broken. "Sometimes, our wishes aren't meant to come true."

Chapter Eighteen

Rory

True night falls and the cave quickly darkens. With no fire, soon it grows so black that I can hardly see my hand in front of my face, let alone Aries. I can hear his breath coming from my left, just a bit too fast for him to be sleeping.

My own breath is coming rapidly, though I try to slow it. My body knows that bad things happen in the dark, and my mind is unable to convince it otherwise. Even curled up on my side in the bedroll, I feel exposed. Somewhere in the cave, I hear the sound of falling gravel and I flinch, banging my elbow into the stone as I crane my head to try to see through the pitch black.

My head knows that it was likely just the wind stirring the dirt but all I can picture is Anik dragging me from my bedroll, and that time Big Jim in the squat woke me by using my back as an ashtray.

"Rory?" Aries speaks suddenly, his voice loud.

"Yeah?" My voice breaks and I swallow against the lump forming inside it. It's irrational, this fear swelling inside me. I have been hurt just as much in the light of day, and even more under the glow of sunlamps, but it is the dark that holds me captive.

"Are you okay?" Aries asks. His hand — *it must be his, who else's could it be?* — lands on my thigh and I flinch, then force myself still.

"Of course," I lie, grateful that I still can, unlike my monster.

"*Angel,*" he corrects me, and I silently apologize.

I don't know if Aries believes me or if he is just unwilling to argue, but he stays silent, the only sound our discordant breathing. His deep and steady, mine quick and shallow.

Closing my eyes, I try to will myself to sleep. The stone beneath me is cold and hard even through the padding but certainly no worse than many of the places I've called home over the years. The Queen's cells were equally cold, and the basement squat in Old York was equally hard.

Sleep evades me.

It is the bugs that find me instead.

I feel their legs crawling over my ankles and up my calves and I kick out, trying to shake them off. Then they are creeping up my waist and I yelp, fighting free of my bedroll to leap to my feet, swatting my hands at every inch of flesh I can find.

My hands touch nothing but skin and clothing but I can't stop myself. My nails, sharp with fear, scratch at my flesh and I open a line of fire on my chest. Then someone — *Aries, it's just Aries* — grabs at my wrists, forcing me still.

"Hey, hey…you're fine, I've got you. I've got you," he reassures me, tugging me against him and squeezing me tight.

"There…there were bugs," I try to explain but I am shivering so hard my teeth clack together. He rubs his hands over my skin, and that, more than anything, convinces me that the bugs are gone, if they were ever there in the first place. Finally, I feel like I can catch a breath, though I'm still shaking.

Gently, like he's holding a piece of glass, he guides me down to his bedroll with him, pulling me into his lap and wrapping himself around me.

"They're gone now," he promises, his hands still soothing me.

"I'm not weak," I tell him, even as I fist my hand in his shirt, clinging to him like a child.

"I think you're the strongest man I know," he answers. Warmth kindles to life inside me. Embarrassed, I turn my face into his chest.

"I don't feel very strong right now. All grown up and still terrified of the dark." My laugh is sharp as broken glass.

"It's not like you don't have cause for it." Aries tightens his arms almost imperceptibly around me.

"I should be used to it by now."

"Why? Does fear have a timeline I'm not aware of?" Aries asks. He tilts my face up. I can't see him—even this close, he is little more than a shadow in the dark, except for his eyes. Like a cat's, they are glowing amber.

"It's illogical." I can't think of anything else to say.

"And does everything have to make sense?" Aries asks, then continues, "Bad things have happened to you in the dark. I doubt that I know of even a fraction of the horrors you've suffered. Your fear is your body's way of trying to keep you safe."

"You sound like a therapist," I grumble, pretending to be upset but inwardly, I'm grateful for his words. Hearing him validate my fear instead of shame me for it somehow helps me chase the terror away. I relax against him.

"I've attended a session or two," Aries admits.

Beneath me, he tenses as if he expects me to make a joke but I don't. Instead, I just settle into a more comfortable position. "Hey, grab my bedroll, will you? We can share it." My words end in a yawn.

He chuckles but drags it over us. "Get some sleep, sweet hart. I'll keep the monsters at bay."

* * * *

Marik

Pain.

It is the first thing Marik feels when he wakes up.

A throbbing hammer fall striking at the base of his skull in time to the beating of his second heart—a commotion of the brain, perhaps, but if so a mild one. His ears are ringing but he remembers being struck in the head by the falling beam.

There is sharp dagger along the right side of his chest—broken ribs, at least one. Marik tentatively draws in a slow breath. All four of his lungs seem fine.

His shoulder is on fire but the pain is already dulling. It must be a soft tissue injury, since his body is already working to heal it.

From his right knee down, he feels…
Nothing.

That, more than the pain, finally forces him to open his eyes. Immediately, he shuts them again, nausea churning in his stomachs. The light above him is too bright, the two suns directly over him in the sky. They leave brilliant orbs dancing across his vision. He blinks away the water filling his eyes.

Marik knows he is stalling. He doesn't want to see, but he refuses to be a coward. He looks.

It's…bad.

His stomach twists violently, threatening to expel its contents all over the rubble that he's partially buried in. His right calf is…the only word for it is mangled. Blood, brilliant and blue, obscures the true depth of the damage.

He sees enough to know that he was exceptionally lucky—he can't feel the pain because one of the cross beams had struck him across his thighs and pinned him, stemming the flow of blood before he could bleed out further.

If he moves it, the bleeding could kill him. If he doesn't, he could lose both his legs and die anyway. Not to mention, he'll be trapped here until he's found. *If* he's found. He'd seen the castle fall. It's hard to imagine that anyone could have survived *that*.

Perhaps the Queen…but if *she* finds him, he knows that he would rather be dead.

Marik gathers his nerve and examines the cross beam. It is thick and sturdy, hardly damaged from the fall. Marik knows he is strong, but he doesn't know if he's strong enough to move it.

This is going to hurt.

It would be easiest to roll it, but that would mean shoving it right onto his lower legs and just the thought of it makes his nausea flare. He takes a deep breath, then coughs as he inhales a lungful of dust and dirt. His vision goes black as it makes every molecule in his body scream with pain.

He curses, breathing slowly now as he attempts to steady himself. He is certain that he received more pain at the Queen's hands, though he can't think of a time at the moment.

"Now or never, Marik," he tells himself, a pep talk that does absolutely nothing to help. Wedging his hands under the beam, he tries to lift it. "Fuck!"

Still cursing, he gives up quickly. The beam hadn't budged and all trying to lift it had done was pull painfully on his already screaming muscles.

So he can't lift it, and trying to roll it off is not an option. Not yet, that would be his last resort. Maybe…maybe he can find something to use as a lever? He looks around, trying to spot anything that might work. *There*! A piece of broken wood. From the scrolling along one side, he can tell it used to be a saddle post. If he can just reach it…

He inches his upper body closer, one tiny painful movement at a time. Stretching as much as he can—far enough he imagines he can feel his skin tearing—he finally brushes the soft wood with the very tips of his fingers. Curling them slowly, he rolls it toward him, one millimeter at a time, until he can grip it. His forehead is covered with sweat and his arms are shaking from the effort, but he has it. Dragging it closer, he drops it right beside his hip.

Marik knows he can't wedge it under the beam yet. He needs to tie off his leg first. If he doesn't, he will bleed out as soon as he's free. If he even manages to free himself before he loses consciousness. Already, he can feel the fuzziness at the edge of his vision.

Carefully, trying not to jostle his leg any more than necessary, he works his belt free from his trousers. By the time he has the leather strap in his hands, he is shaking and sweaty, breath ragged as if he'd just fought a duel.

And maybe he had—a duel against himself and time.

He cinches the belt low on his right thigh, just above where the beam keeps it pinned, tightening it until he is crying out with pain, then grabs for the broken saddle post. Wedging it under the beam as close to his hip as he can, he tries to shift it.

It budges, but not enough. He needs more leverage. He needs...a fulcrum. He spots a broken bridle rack just out of reach. But maybe...if he uses the saddle post...

He manages to slide it close enough to grab and drag it into position. The angle is awkward but Marik is persistent. For the first time in his existence, he is grateful for the pain training the Queen has put him through—without it, he does not think he would have the fortitude to do what needs to be done.

He frees what is left of his leg.

The belt stops him from bleeding out but does nothing to dim the agony that roars through him like a wildfire.

He doesn't want to look but he knows he doesn't have a choice. If he passes out here, he will die, and he is not ready to be planted. Not here, not like this. He breathes in through his nose, then out through his mouth, then repeats it until his hands are no longer shaking.

Then, he forces himself to look again. His tibia is visibly broken just below his right knee, blue-stained bone poking out from shredded skin. It is even worse than he thought it was earlier. No healer could repair this amount of damage, not even on one of his kind.

Already, he can see the wound struggling to heal. If he lets it, he will be crippled permanently. Better to remove it cleanly, he knows. He has seen many a wound like this—or worse—on the battlefield. He's seen the way they can turn honorable warriors into withered, wasted men. Little better than humans, unable to walk without limping, their deformities ugly to the eyes.

He'd rather wear a prosthetic. It is not a lie…but it is not wholly the truth, either. No prosthetic, no matter how well crafted, no matter how much magic is poured into it, could ever respond the way his own flesh and blood does.

But his own flesh and blood is no longer an option.

Before he can talk himself out of it, he draws his dagger. Already, the numbness is wearing off as blood tries to return to his extremities. His left leg is filling with static, stinging pins and needles. His right…

There is little feeling, proof again that he couldn't save it even if he wants to. *At least*, he thinks as he hunches over his knee, *the bone is already broken.*

He presses the sharp edge of his blade against the still-connected sinew and cuts through it once, then again. It takes four slices in total before his calf falls to the ground. The sawed-off stump is ugly but the belt is keeping most of the bleeding at bay.

A wave of weakness floods his body as his healing speeds up, struggling to keep him alive. Fresh new skin, pink and tender, knits itself across the exposed tissue. Only when it is finally closed does he allow himself to sag back and loosen the belt.

Tears sting his eyes. *They are not a sign of weakness,* he tells himself, even as shame burns at his throat.

It is done.

He allows himself a single moment to mourn the loss, then forces himself onto his knees. Once he is free of the rubble, he can summon Aphid.

Fifteen feet.

He cannot stand, but he can crawl.

Twice, he puts his hand down on an exposed nail and twice more rubble shifts, threatening to rebury him, but finally, he reaches the grass. He nearly sobs, no longer caring if he appears weak, as he touches the soft, warm blades. Marik collapses to his side, breath ragged. On his knees, the distance that he'd normally cross in seconds had taken longer, and things that should be effortless had left him panting.

And every movement had sent agony through his still-healing body. He is exhausted, drained of not only his energy but his will to move. Surely, he can take a moment to rest.

Maybe he falls asleep, or maybe he just closes his eyes for a while, he's not certain. All he knows is that suddenly, he hears the grass bending as quiet footsteps approach from the south and his eyes snap open.

He tries to stand but only makes it to his knees before a booted foot strikes him in the chest, sending him tumbling back onto his ass.

"Well, well, well…what do we have here?"

Hearts pounding, Marik looks up—and up—into the smirking face of the looming man. His veins fill with ice as he recognizes him.

"How is this possible?" Marik asks.

The man laughs.

Chapter Nineteen

Aries

Rory is going to kill *me,* I think as I stare up the length of the silver blade pointed between my eyes to the creature holding it, *if they don't do it first.*

I hadn't seen them enter the cave. In fact, somehow, I hadn't seen them at all until they'd appeared, as if out of thin air, in a semi-circle around us. Seven strangers in total, all armed. With only the light of the moon filtering in from outside the cave to see by, my eyes are straining to pick up details.

Rory is still asleep against me. I know that I should wake him, but I'm afraid of what the boy would do if he awakens like this, surrounded by what can only be enemies.

The creatures are certainly not the high fae I am used to seeing. While on Earth, I'd grown used to seeing fellow Sidhe, as they were the only ones permitted a travel visa. And before I'd walked through the tear, I'd spent most of my years in the Sidhe Court or fighting with the Sidhe armies. My mother prioritizes beauty over anything. Any fae who did not fit her standards was executed or banished, depending on her mood.

Creatures like these would never be permitted inside the boundaries of Undying Spring.

They are beast-like, though they stand on two legs like a man. But, unlike a man, their legs end in hooves that remind me of a mountain goat. Their pale fur is thick, ideal for cold mountain nights, and covers every inch of their bodies from mid-chest down. Their hands are close enough to a man's to be able to hold a sword.

Their heads, though, are grotesque — once I look at the nearest, I can't pull my gaze away.

They have no eyes, and it is clear to me immediately that they were born this way. Where the eyes should be instead is just smooth, pulsing, nearly translucent flesh. Unlike the fur on their bodies, their heads are covered only sparsely with what looks more like antennae than hair. Their mouths are almost humanoid, but when the one with the sword opens it to chatter at me, I see they have no teeth, just strange, bonelike ridges.

I don't recognize the language, but the sound is loud enough to startle Rory awake. I grab for him, clasping him back to my chest before he can lunge accidentally toward any of the strangers.

"What —" Rory yelps, but I shush him. Rory goes still as stone against me, his body strung tight. His gaze is flicking around the cave, like he's not sure where to look for danger, then one of the beasts moves, his hoof clicking on the stone, and Rory's gaze locks toward the sound.

The creature chatters again, jerking the sword up in a manner that obviously means for us to stand. Slowly,

I push myself to my feet. Keeping a tight hold on Rory, I angle him behind me as much as I can.

With the sword, the creature gestures toward the back of the cave, which I can now see has changed. Where I am certain before was solid stone now opens to a tunnel. If these creatures lived beneath the earth, then the lack of eyes makes sense to me. What use are eyes when there is no light to see by?

This doesn't bode well for us.

The creature, clearly frustrated by my lack of speed in obeying, prods at me with the tip of the sword, proving to me that, not only is it sharp, but the beings can somehow still sense us enough to be dangerous even without eyes.

"Can I grab our things?" I try to ask, speaking slowly, but the creature shrieks at me, jabbing at me harder with the sword. I barely manage to avoid being skewered. I know that Rory can likely see nothing. He'd have no way to dodge if they were to stab toward him instead.

Can I fight my way through them? Perhaps, but not without possible injury and definitely not without risking Rory's life. Each of the creatures is taller than me by at least a head and nearly twice as broad, and every inch of them appears to be solid muscle.

Best to try to lose them in the tunnels, I think, *and hope we can find our way back to the surface*. Thankfully, Rory seems to be on the same page as me. He doesn't speak, but he clings to my side as we start to move toward the darker passageway. Beyond the mouth of the tunnel — *clearly no natural formation, it is too smooth to be anything but formed by hand* – it is completely without light.

I know that I couldn't possibly have missed it during my initial evaluation of the cave. I'd done a thorough walkthrough specifically to avoid this exact situation. The tunnel must have been hidden in some way — likely, I assume, by magic. There was no evidence of a doorway that could have been carefully crafted and moved out of the way.

I should have sensed it.

More than that, Faerie should have warned me.

Why hadn't she?

Silently, I reach out to her...then nearly panic when I sense nothing.

What the fuck is going on?

The chattering beast jabs me in the back with the tip of his sword, hard enough I feel it pierce my skin, and I hiss. It takes every scrap of courage I possess to step into the inky blackness with Rory at my side but whatever waits us there, it is better than certain death here.

I hear the creatures surround us in the dark, their steps smooth. Clearly, the creatures don't need light to navigate, but Rory and I are immediately blind. We stumble over each other but neither are willing to step further away.

I can tell from the sound of their chattering that the creatures are displeased at our slow speed but without light, we can't move any faster. Already, I am walking with my arm thrust in front of us to avoid running into another wall when the tunnel turns. And the ground, though worn smoother than I would expect, slopes downward just steeply enough for me to struggle to keep my balance, and Rory seems to be having a worse time of it than me. He's fallen once already, scuffing his palms. I can scent his blood on the air.

It fuels my anger, especially when I can feel the creatures draw closer, their bodies radiating heat in the steadily colder air. How deep are we descending? And how long can we go before the chill becomes too much? It was cold enough at the surface, now the air bites at my skin and Rory doesn't have shoes.

Even the air has grown heavier, thicker, making it hard to draw in a full breath.

Then, Rory stumbles again, and this time, he doesn't get up.

I holler, dropping to my knees at his side, trying to shake him awake but then I feel it too, a sudden wave of weakness. I try to fight it without success. I feel my body slump beside his before my vision goes black.

* * * *

I wake alone.

That, not the cage I am trapped in, is what makes me panic.

Where is Rory? I twist, banging my knees into the solid iron bars. I hiss, jerking away from the toxic metal, but it doesn't stop me from looking for Rory. Unfortunately, it is immediately clear that I am alone in the cage. There would be no room for another person in here no matter how closely we tried to lie. The pen's ceiling is so low that I smack one of my antlers into it when I try to sit up. The air fills with the scent of burning hair.

My eyes are blurry and out of focus when I try to peer through the bars of the pen. I rub at them, blinking them clear, then try again. They are slow to focus but when they do, what I see chills me to the bone.

I can tell from the softly glowing stalactites along the roof of the cavern that I am still under the mountain. The silver-veined stone floor is covered in frost. It is no longer dark thanks to the many blue-flamed torches that had been hung evenly along the walls. The light illuminates the cages.

Hundreds of them, just like mine.

All that I can see have been crafted of pure iron, a terrifying realization. How did the creatures come by it? They were fae, that much I had been able to tell, so they certainly hadn't been able to craft the pens themselves.

I put the thought away to dwell on later, scanning each of the cages that I can see, looking for Rory. I don't want to see him trapped like me, but if he's not here...then where is he?

I see sprites and dyrads and wood elves — and, most terrifying of all, at least a dozen high fae like me. Each and every one of them should have the power of a dozen lesser fae combined. If they haven't managed to escape, it doesn't bode well for Rory and me.

The more I look, the worse things seem.

All of them look broken. Some physically — I see a centaur that has been forced to kneel on a clearly broken leg, and a nymph so disfigured that she's difficult to look at — but even the ones who appear uninjured have a blankness in their eyes.

But no matter where I look, I don't see Rory.

"Don't bother," a craggy voice sounds from the pixie in the cage beside me. I turn to stare at him. He is small and slender, like much of his kind. I flinch at the scars that line his face. His species is known for their playfulness and sweet temper. They tend the gardens and the lakes. I'd never seen one so much as hold gardening shears, let alone a weapon. To see one bearing the mark of war? It's...unnatural.

"Don't bother what?" I ask, fearing his answer.

"Looking for whoever you came with. They keep us separate so we don't try to escape," the pixie answers.

"Who are 'they'? What do they want?" I ask, for some reason feeling the need to lower my voice though I haven't spotted any signs of guards.

The pixie shrugs. "What the Unsidhe bastards always want. Blood and pain and a spectacle."

Unsidhe...so we made it to our destination. I had considered what we would do when we got to its border, but I had thought we'd have more time to make a plan. I'd known there was a possibility that the court would not be pleasant to me but I *had* thought we'd have the opportunity to at least plead our case. Or *Rory's* case, anyway.

"How long have they held you? Is there any way out?" As I ask, I scan the cavern for clues, for anything that could be of use. There's nothing. I see frost on the walls and ice patches on the walkways but nothing that I could use as a weapon, not even an icicle.

The pixie barks out a laugh. "Oh, there's a way out. Give in and die. Otherwise, there's just this. Fight, fuck, then do it again the next day. In the time I've been here, none have escaped and any who try...they live to regret it." The pixie's wings flutter, betraying his agitation before he adds, "But all of them wish they hadn't. As for how long? How does one tell time without the sun or growing things? I was small when they grabbed me, the youngest in my troupe, and now I am this." He stands, tall enough his golden curls almost brush the top of his cage. At three feet tall, he is as tall as many of his brethren get. Fully grown, or almost.

Considering how long it takes pixies to age...I shudder. If he was truly a child when taken, he must have been here since the fall of Morrigan, or shortly after. How had I not heard of this? Raids by the Unsidhe…my mother should have stepped in.

I turn to stare at the other caged faeries, an icy fist around my heart. "And all of them…the Unsidhe took them?" Surely that can't be the case. One raid, two…I could see how they could be missed. Most fae are transient creatures and it's not like we complete a census. But…there have to be hundreds just in this cavern alone.

The pixie gives me a funny look. "Some of them were taken during raids, but the Queen sold the rest."

"Sold?" I practically shout the word, not wanting to believe that my mother, corrupt though she may be, would be willing to sell her own people. "For what?"

The pixie shrugs. "You'd have to ask her."

If I ever lay eyes on her again, I certainly plan to… I clench my hand into a fist, wishing for my sword. My mother has much to answer for.

Chapter Twenty

Rory

Furry, bipedal mole-rats.

I wake surrounded by them. From the sound of their chattering, I know these ugly creatures are the things that had surrounded us back in the cave, the beasts that had urged us down into a tunnel that shouldn't have existed in the first place. It had been too dark for me to see them then and I find myself wishing for the dark now.

Not truly, especially now that I know what they look like — the thought of being surrounded by them in pitch blackness makes me shiver. It is bad enough when I can see them.

"Stay back!" I holler as the nearest one steps closer. Angel and I are sharing my body at the moment, something I wasn't aware was possible. Normally, one of us is closer to the surface than the other. He swipes our long, venomous claws at it.

The creature freezes in place. It has already seen—well, not seen, considering the lack of fucking eyes—learned of the dangers of coming too close. While I can't control the toxins my claws produce, Angel apparently can, which explains why none of my scratches have ever affected Aries like this.

The mole-man I'd scratched—and I'd only barely caught the skin along his jaw before he'd jerked out of reach again—had immediately collapsed. I'd watched his body stiffen, muscles twitching, before his pale skin started changing color. Along the edge of the barely inch-long scratch, his flesh had started to rot in front of me.

Perhaps his companions can't see him, but they'd sure as shit heard him start to scream and I'd guarantee their sense of smell is better than mine. It had been several moments since the mole-man died and I can still smell the wound's decay.

The mole-men chatter to each other, retreating back to the mouth of the tunnel. I take a moment to look around again. I hadn't gotten many options since I'd woken, surrounded by the creatures who were clearly trying to get me to go somewhere with them.

I have no intention of being taken anywhere, unless it's to Aries.

I'm inside a small grotto. Maybe six or seven paces from one side to the other, and the same from the back wall where I'm standing to the tunnel. The walls are jagged, convincing me that this is likely a naturally formed cave that they've repurposed into a cell of some sort. The gate is currently open. I vaguely remember that it was the sound of it opening that woke me. The silver hinges were quiet but the wood had creaked.

There's no way out beside the door. Even if I climb the uneven walls — there are plenty of handholds — the ceiling isn't high enough to keep me out of reach and there are no air holes or vents to take advantage of. Which sucks, because now that I'm looking, I see the orange-red dust covering everything. Even my skin is coated in it.

It has no smell, I realize when I try to identify it. I stick out my tongue to taste it when Angel takes control of my body. I sense his exasperation as he says, *"Don't lick the iron dust, you idiot."*

"It's not like it will hurt you," I point out, no longer interested in tasting the dirt. He's making it sound like I wanted to lick it in the first place.

"It's not going to help us either."

Before I can argue back, one of the mole-men in the tunnel barks. Then I hear bare feet — not hooves — on the stone. One of the mole-men chatters at the new arrival. A moment later, a terrified-looking human steps through the gate.

I go to lower my hands but Angel stops me, raising them again. *"It could be a trick,"* he says, and I know he is right. The boy may look young — if he has gone through puberty yet, I'll eat my hat — but that doesn't mean anything in Faerie. Some of the most dangerous changelings used to be the young. They hadn't yet learned the hard truth that no matter how like the fae they became, they would always, *always* be second class.

"Th-they say you are t-to come with them," the boy translates for me.

I roll my eyes. "I got that." They'd repeated the order a half-dozen times already. The reason I'm still in the grotto isn't because I don't understand them, though their voices are guttural.

The boy looks over his shoulder, cringing as the mole-man waves him on. When he looks back into the cave, his eyes land on the dead mole-man and he yelps, stumbling back against the wall, away from the body. He swallows hard, then looks at me again.

"Tell them I'm not going anywhere until I see Aries," I repeat the same thing I'd told them the first time they'd tried to talk me out of the cave.

Behind the boy, one of the mole-man chitters.

"They said that there is no Aries here. Just you."

"And I said that I don't *fucking* believe them."

It seems we are still at an impasse. I can't fight them off forever, I'm not stupid enough to believe that, but I can certainly make them hurt in the meantime. Eventually, I will need to sleep and they likely have an endless number of beasts to rotate out with. They can outlast me...but I have no plans to make this easy on them.

Considering the smallness of the cave, they can't overwhelm me with numbers and none of them are willing to come within arms' reach of me, at least not at the moment. I have the upper hand.

Until one of the mole-men returns with a poleax.

* * * *

"It could be worse," I tell Angel but I am really trying to convince myself. The fact that it's true is only a small consolation.

It appears that the Unsidhe have better sport than torturing humans. Instead, any changelings like me who wander into their domain have been put to work. Mining, of all things, iron.

What did the faerie bastards want with it? None of the changelings in my work team have any idea. Apparently, like me, they'd woken in a cave and been put to work immediately.

We get two meals a day—bread and rancid meat, I try not to think where it comes from, or what creature it had been when it lived. I suspect, from the way the mole-men were speaking when they dragged away the corpse of a changeling, his head caved in by a fallen rock, that it was better not to know.

But the mole-men don't withhold water. We get as much as we ask for. I'd learned quickly, though, not to ask for too much. I'd guzzled it, out of breath and exhausted, the first water break and made myself sick. I'd thrown up what looked like mud. Apparently, I'd breathed in so much dust that the water mixed with it in my belly too.

I'm beginning to feel like I'll never be clean again. It's so thick on my skin, I can't help but compare myself to an Oompa-Loompa.

I swing my hammer against the ore deposit for what must be the thousandth time today. There's no way to tell time down here. We're not even let out to eat. Instead, the mole-men collect our hammers and chisels—wouldn't do, apparently, to leave us with something that could be used as a weapon, even if we are clearly too exhausted to make use of them—and order us to sit down right here in the tunnels with our measly meal.

I couldn't have been down here much longer than a day and already I'm coughing.

Fucking iron dust.

I swing my hammer again, finally loosening the deposit enough that large chunks of stone ore clatter to the tunnel ground. Immediately, one of the grimdelins—what the mole-men are called, apparently—rushes forward, shoving me out of the way so a different changeling can gather them up.

I'm not sure how they decide which of us should have certain jobs, but they've split us up in some way that makes sense only to them. Some of us break the rock, some of us gather the ore, some of us light fires against the walls in between to soften it. And the youngest of us carry skins of water to the workers.

I hate looking at the children.

They have dead eyes.

"Keep working!" one of the grimdelins barks at me, and reluctantly, I swing my hammer again.

There is frost on the ceiling and ice on the floors—it melts when we build the fires, then refreezes, but I am not cold. Instead, I feel like I am burning, from my shoulders and thighs to my face. I have a fever. Maybe it is from the back-breaking work, maybe from the spoiled food. In the end, it doesn't matter.

How have the others survived this, I wonder? At lunch, or whatever meal we'd been given, I'd spoken to a few of them, the ones who were willing to talk. Which had been too few of them, compared to the number of us down here. Most of the changelings seem...hollow inside. Shells, bodies that move and work but...no lights on upstairs, as it were.

Maybe they could be saved someday, if they were free of this place. I'd certainly been no better back in the Sidhe Court, trapped under the influence of *Salvia*.

I swing my hammer again.

There's no use thinking of it now anyway. We're not free and no matter how Angel and I have looked, we can't find a way to get free either. There's only one way out of the mine. Not only is it kept gated and locked, but the silver bars visibly spark with strands of violet magic that strengthen them against any attempts to break them, or so the de facto leader of the changelings, Haylen, told me. And even if we take out all the grimdelins down here with us, the only key to open the gate is kept with the guard outside it.

Apparently, some of the changelings had tried to take over the mine once before, using the grimdelins inside as hostages. The creatures didn't care. They'd fired arrows into the mine through the gates, killing the hostages themselves, then left them without food until they'd grown so weak there had been no fighting back when they'd finally opened the gates and flooded the mine with new guards.

We are stuck here.

I don't allow myself to wonder what they are doing to Aries. He's a faerie...surely they are treating him better than this? Surely...

I can't help but remember the way Queen Nuala had treated the only Unsidhe fae I'd ever laid eyes on, a scout with the wings of an eagle her guards had trapped in the forest along the borders. She'd carved off his wings and skinned him, then sent him — still living — back to his King as a warning.

Would the King retaliate?

"Fuck!" I swing my hammer as hard as I can against the walls, accidentally triggering a small avalanche of ore to tumble down. It crashes with the strength of dozens of thrown fists against my calves and I drop my hammer as I stumble back.

Down the tunnel, a similar avalanche starts but that changeling isn't as lucky. The stones that fall on him are larger and he is left partially buried. I wait for the changelings on either side of him to turn and help but they keep working, completely ignoring the fallen man.

"Fuck this shit," I growl, dropping my hammer as I race toward him.

Before I reach him, though, a mole-man steps in my way and plants his hands on my chest, shoving me back. I stumble, tripping over a rock and falling on my ass.

"Get...to work," he barks out the order.

"He needs help!" I argue, pushing myself to my feet, claws elongated in threat.

"No...help. You have...quota. Work or...no food for whole mine," the grimdelin threatens and I hear the sincerity in his voice.

"Bastard," I grumble but reluctantly return to my post, understanding now why the others didn't bother trying to help.

I understand, but I hate it.

Chapter Twenty-One

Rory

The grimdelins finally call an end to our work. We'd met our mysterious quota and are allowed to pass over our weapons. I turn toward the crushed changeling, fearing what I'll see, but the others near him have already started to carefully unbury him.

I am surprised to find him still breathing.

Later, as we tear into the rotted meat, Haylen explains it to me in a quiet, too-calm voice. "I don't know how it is in your Sidhe Court, but here, Faerie does not care about us. The only reason she won't allow us to die is because our hands can do the labor that her precious fae cannot. They cannot dig the ore from the ground. They couldn't even breathe the air down here."

"About that," I ask, frowning as the thought comes to me. "The mole-men — grimdelins, I mean. How can they stand it down here? The iron, it's everywhere."

"They aren't fae. Or at least, not full-blooded. I don't know what they are. They must have at least a bit of fae blood in them, because they definitely don't like to handle the iron, but it doesn't hurt them the way it does the true ones," Haylen answers.

"What do they do with the ore once we break it free?" I ask. I can't think of a single use for it here.

Oh, for us changelings, sure. If we had the right tools, we could forge it into weapons and become a truly unstoppable army. No faerie could stand against us with iron in our hands...

But for faeries? It would be useless.

"I know some of it is forged into kennels. A few of us have been rotated to that duty once or twice." Haylen shrugs. "Not sure if they use it for anything else or if we're just getting rid of it so it's not *here*."

I go to ask another question — *what are the kennels for?* — but the man from earlier, the one who'd been crushed, lets loose a loud, agonized scream. One of the other changelings rushes over, bending down to mutter something I can't hear into Haylen's ear.

His shoulders slump but he nods, seemingly reluctant. When he looks at me, his eyes are filled with pain. "This won't be pleasant to watch. You might want to turn away."

With those parting words, he stands and moves to the crushed changeling's side. Once there, he crouches, speaking to the man for a few moments. The broken man nods, seemingly frantic.

I can't look away, not even when Haylen wraps his hands around the man's fragile throat and strangles him.

* * * *

Aries

From the pixie in the cage next to mine, I learn many things — but not how to escape.

I learn that he goes by Sage, and that the other prisoners call him Prophet. Apparently, he has an uncanny ability to tell which fighters will return from the arena…and which will die.

I learn that the creatures who Rory and I stumbled on are called grimdelins, and that they patrol the tunnels surrounding the Court Under the Mountain. I also learn that the only time we get let out of the cages is to fight in the arena if we're lucky, or to lay with the spectators if we are not.

I have no intention of complying with either.

I quickly learn that I have little choice in the matter.

They come for me in my sleep.

I stay awake as long as I can, despite Sage's urging that I will need my rest, but I can't avoid sleeping forever. It feels like I've barely closed my eyes when they are dragging me out of the cell, prodding at me with lightning rods until I am on my feet. The ground is slippery and twice I almost fall.

Before I can do more than throw a punch, one of the grimdelin's manages to hook a garrote around my neck, pulling it tight until I'm forced to stand still or slice my own throat. I can't risk it—not without knowing where Rory is and what he is suffering. I have little hope that he is being treated well. From my time spent watching, I have learned that here, in the Court Under the Mountain, even the Unsidhe are not safe from treachery.

Several times, fae in fancy robes have walked along the pens, 'admiring' the fighters. I'd heard them speak of their plots against their enemies, the many ways they planned to betray their lovers…once, I'd even seen one stabbed in the back by his companion.

No…Rory would be no safer here than in my mother's care.

The grimdelin behind me kicks my calf.

"Walk," it orders, the word barely understandable. It doesn't loosen the garrote. When I swallow, I feel the metal bite into my skin.

Slowly, I start to move. It takes everything in my power not to pull against it. If it weren't for Rory being trapped somewhere here, I'd take the risk and do it — but if I die, he will be stuck here forever.

I should have taken the risk and fought back in the cave, rather than hoping for a better opportunity. Or better yet, found a way to get him back to Earth instead of going along with his plan to plead asylum from the Unsidhe. Clearly, they are no better than the bitch we are fleeing from.

The grimdelin force-marches me to a larger pen, shoving me inside. He scuttles out, slamming the heavy door between us before I can do more than growl.

The pixie had explained this too. The faeries that are chosen to fight get shoved into holding pens on either side of the arena. When they are ready for us, they'll open the gate — I scan the walls until I see it, on the other side of the empty room from the door — and let us in.

He'd warned me not to linger in the pen. Apparently, plenty of the conscripted fighters didn't feel like fighting — imagine that. If we take too long to give the watchers a show, they'll flood the pen with scurion, venomous spider-like crustaceans whose bites apparently feel worse than the kiss of iron.

I wish I had my sword but I remind myself that it won't be the first time I've entered a fight unarmed. Arteria had warned me not to rely on my weapon. How many times had he accosted Anik and I in the corridors without warning?

Whatever I face on the other side of this gate—*whoever* I face—I cannot allow them to win. If I'm to find Rory and escape, I must do whatever it takes to survive.

The gate opens.

I run through, taking in as much of my surroundings as I can while my eyes seek for my opponent. The cavern floor has been covered in snow that shifts beneath my boots like sand. The arena walls are carved from ice—too smooth to climb and too tall to jump, keeping the beastly fae in the stands safe from my reach, if I were to try to attack them.

Large boulders are scattered through the arena seemingly at random, providing ample places to hide, and my opponent must be behind one of them because I don't spot him immediately.

Just as I think that, the snow in front of me explodes. It stings my eyes and while I'm blinking them clear, my opponent attacks. A naga, I realize, as I barely dodge her lunge. She's unarmed like me, but her nails are long and sharp as thorns.

Hissing, she lands on her belly, her arms dragging her across the snow like a lyndwyrm as she turns to chase me. I run for a boulder, frantically planning my attack. Her natural weapons are better than mine—even if I could pull on a glamour, something I haven't been able to do since crossing into Faerie. I wish I knew why. She'd never stopped me before. But she'd never gone silent on me like this before, either. It seems that, for whatever reason, she's abandoned me.

She's fast, moving through the snow as if it is water. I certainly can't outlast her. I'll wear myself out well before she will exhaust herself. Eventually, the cold might slow her down but not quickly enough. Unlike her smaller brethren, the naga are warm blooded. Her heat is already melting the snow where she crosses it, turning it to ice as it refreezes.

My best chance is to somehow get behind her.

I dart to the left as she lunges again, narrowly avoiding her gnashing jaws. Her teeth, I can now see, are long and narrow, curved like a viper's fangs. They glint in the torchlight.

Venomous, of course she is. I curse as I duck out of her way again, then I see it. My opportunity. She crashes back to the snow but when she tries to get her hands underneath her again, one palm slips against the ice.

I leap onto her back, resting my weight on the part of her spine just where the tail formed, pinning her in place. It won't keep her still for long—already, her muscles are bunching beneath me and I can feel her gathering her strength.

But I don't need long. Just long *enough.* I catch her in a blood choke, snaking my right arm around her neck to grab my own shoulder, then use my left against the back of her neck, pushing her head farther down. Nine seconds. That's all it takes before her body sags into the snow.

I could release her now, and she would live—but she would almost definitely wake up and keep fighting. Instead, I harden my heart, keeping hold until I feel the life leave her.

To get Rory back and safe, I would trade the world.

One naga's life is not keeping me from him.

For the first time since entering the arena, I hear the crowd. They go wild, screaming and pounding their fists, stomping their feet until the cavern fills with the sound of thunder.

I let the naga's body drop, then look up at the stands, scanning each face until I see him. The Fomorian sitting alone on a throne of stone and ice, staring down at me with dark eyes and a sharp smile.

The Unsidhe King.

King Adalberon

The fight did not take nearly as long as he expected and had been won without the spilling of a single drop of blood. He finds this...disappointing. The naga is — *was*, he corrects himself — his prized fighter, his undefeated champion. If she were to die, he'd hoped it to be a grand spectacle, something that would keep his court talking for centuries.

He certainly hadn't expected this unassuming, unarmed faerie to end her in minutes. The high fae appears average in all ways — not particularly tall or broad, his only natural weapons the average-sized rack of antlers sprouting from his dark curls, not sharp enough to be much of a threat and unwieldy enough he would have expected them to be a liability.

It isn't often the new arrivals manage to surprise him.

The faerie fighter, still perched over his fallen foe, lifts his gaze to scan the crowd. When he meets Adalberon's eyes, the King expects to see fear.

Instead, he sees a threat.

Adalberon smirks, lounging back in his throne with little care. The new fighters always have such...*spirit* about them. He enjoys watching them break. It won't be long and this one will break too.

Adalberon looks closer, then frowns.

This one seems...familiar.

Adalberon leans down to speak to his herald, a Cait-sith with particularly striking coloring. His fur is a violet so dark it is nearly black, and he has a voice that

Adalberon finds pleasing. Currently, he is in his bipedal form. A cat-boy, the humans would call him, with large ears and a flicking tail that makes a perfect handle when Adalberon fucks him.

Nyx listens to Adalberon's words, then nods, stepping toward the edge of the stadium box to call down to the fighter, "Our Great and Majestic King, the Lord of Winter, Prince of Frost and Ruler of Twilight, is pleased by the fighter's skill in combat. He bids you welcome to his arena and wishes you a more spectacular death than you dealt in your next battle."

The faerie clearly hears the threat underlying the herald's words, as does the crowd—they scream their excitement from a thousand throats—but it doesn't cow him. Instead, the fighter stands and struts closer to the Royal Box. His spine is straight, his head high.

He calls up, "King Adalberon! I have heard rumors of your greatness. I see that they have been largely...exaggerated."

Immediately, rage fills Adalberon's chest. This puny faerie dares to mock *him*? Adalberon is the last of the Formorians, second in strength to none within these halls! This...*weakling*...is lucky that the King is as merciful as he is cunning. He will not order him stripped and skinned alive for his impertinence. *Yet.*

His herald, though, squeaks, darting his gaze back to Adalberon as he visibly cowers. Adalberon dismisses the insult with a wave of his hand. "Tell him that we are amused."

As usual, Nyx understands more than what Adalberon says. When he speaks, it is as if he pulled the words directly from the King's mind. "Our Great and Majestic King finds your impertinence amusing, but would caution the fighter to mind his words if he enjoys having the future use of his tongue."

"I would challenge the King to come take it himself, if he has even half the courage and fortitude the stories claim." The dark-skinned faerie, Adalberon realizes, is serious.

The stones on him!

King Adalberon laughs and waves his herald back. He leans forward in his throne and speaks directly down to him, "You are unarmed, yet you think to challenge *me*? I would use your rib bones as a toothpick. I would garnish my supper with your knucklebones! Little warrior, you are funny! What do they call you in the Land of Endless Thaw?"

"I have gone by many names. Why should I share any of them with you?" The faerie cocks his head, looking much like the deer his antlers belong on. There's something sharp behind his eyes that keeps Adalberon on edge.

"You would rather die nameless?" Adalberon asks, genuinely curious.

"I do not intend to die," the faerie answers, his spine straight. For a second, Adalberon sees a green and gold circlet on his head and a dark shadow looming behind him, taller and broader of shoulder, before it is gone.

For the first time in eons, unease prickles along Adalberon's skin.

The prophecy settles on his shoulders like a shroud. His vision goes white.

Two armies on the ice.

Snow stained by spilled blood.

Adalberon's crown, bouncing down the rocky face of the mountain.

This man, this nameless faerie, will be the downfall of his kingdom if he stays here. Faerie had not told him how, or when…but he feels the truth of the prophecy in his bones.

Adalberon leans down to his herald. "Have him sent to my chambers. Make sure he is bound thrice, and he is not to be left alone."

"Yes, Your Majesty."

Chapter Twenty-Two

Aries

One moment, I am verbally sparing with the King. The next, his eyes grow white and he is no longer amused. His smirk slides from his face like water, leaving behind a blank nothing. It sends a shiver of unease down my spine and I clench my hands, wishing again for a sword.

The King waves his hand and, immediately, four grimdelins leap down from the stadium and into the arena. They quickly encircle me. For a second, I am back in the cave, but this time, I am prepared to fight.

Before I can, the herald calls down, "The King will entertain you in his chambers." The audience boos, several Unsidhe standing and beginning their trek to the exits. Clearly, they know that the show is over. For now, anyway.

A private audience with the King is likely the best chance I have of convincing him to let me see Rory — and hopefully, to let us go. Even if I don't succeed, I can learn valuable information about the layout of the court.

I lower my fists and reluctantly allow them to bind me with leather cuffs, hemp rope and silver chains. Everything inside me strains to rip them off, to fight back before they can completely incapacitate me, but I hold steady.

I have to trust that there will be an opportunity again. Though I can't reach her, I whisper a prayer to Faerie regardless, begging her to keep Rory safe no matter what happens to me. As I expect, she is silent.

One of the grimdelins drops a dark-colored sack over my head before dragging me from the arena, not seeming to care if his rough handling means I trip. Thankfully for me, I keep my feet under me despite the ice. Even better, the lack of eyesight has little effect on the mental map I'm building of the Court.

It had been another of Arteria's exercises, though he'd blinded us by more imaginative means than a bag over our heads. By the time we stop, I know exactly how to get from the pens to the arena, and from the arena to the King's quarters. I'm one step closer to finding an escape route.

When we finally stop, the bag is yanked from my head. It gets caught on one of the tines of my antlers and I hear it tear, then the grimdelin to my left is slapped over the head by another. I'm beginning to notice differences between them now that I've watched them more.

I get the impression that the first is younger. The wrinkles beside his eyes are not quite as deep, his skin a shade darker. The other stands taller. He chatters at the younger one and I suspect, though I don't understand the language, that he is scolding him.

So. They have a chain of command. I file the information away then look around. I don't know what I expect. Something like my mother's chambers, perhaps — gaudy tapestries, gold and jewels as far as the eye can see. Instead, it is militarian. I am brought to a large, circular sitting room. The marble floor is bare and even here, there is frost upon it. The oval table is bare and the couch is nearly as hard as stone when I am shoved on it to wait.

One of the grimdelins chatters a warning at me. I ignore him.

This may be my only chance to speak to the King. I can't waste it.

When he enters, I stand and force myself to angle my head respectfully, careful not to aim my antlers at him by accident. I cannot risk him taking it as a threat, even if I am still bound.

"Your Majesty," I greet him.

"You are an enigma, dark fighter," King Adalberon says as he crosses the room to the chair opposite me. "Sit. Let us discuss your situation."

Slowly, I sit, keeping my eyes on him. "I came with another. I would know of his condition."

"In time, perhaps," King Adalberon says easily. "Answer my questions and I will consider answering yours."

I know I am not in a place to bargain, but it goes against my nature to do otherwise. I would bury my pride if I thought it would save Rory but I get the sense that in this situation it would doom us both.

I trust my instincts.

"Answer for answer," I propose. "A fair trade."

The King stares at me as he considers it. Finally, he nods. "Swear that you will answer honestly and I will do the same."

Does he not realize that I cannot lie? I wonder. I'd heard that the Fomorians were not bound by the Sooth but I'd thought it a myth. And since they'd been nearly eradicated, I'd never given it much thought beyond that.

"So I swear," I promise, but add, "to be honest in any question I choose to answer from now until…" I pause, looking around until my gaze lands on the perfect object sitting on the only bookshelf, "the sands of that hourglass have stopped falling." From the speed they are trickling down, I can estimate that will give us a half hour, maybe a bit more. Without a time limit, I worry he will keep me here answering questions for an eternity.

I am not careless enough to promise an answer to every question he asks. The Unsidhe King is an unknown to me. There is no telling what tricks he may try.

The King's eyes flash with something like approval, then he nods his head. "With your conditions, I so swear." He leans back in his chair, then asks his first question. "By what name do I know you? The shape of your face is familiar to me."

It is the question I feared he would ask but had already prepared myself to answer. I know I am taking a risk—our two Courts have never been friendly. He could choose to order my death as soon as my name leaves my lips. But if I want answers about Rory's condition, it is a risk I must take.

"You may know me as Aries or Aodhan," I answer, giving him the name I have chosen for myself now as well as the name I chose before leaving for Earth. Neither are my true name, but that is one he would not have known anyway, so it is not a lie.

As I suspect, it is my old name he mutters to himself, brows lowered. "Aodhan..." Suddenly, his eyes sharpen as he meets mine. "Ah, yes. The Bloody Prince. My armies learned much from the teachings of your sword during the War."

It is not the first time I have heard that title. I removed the heads from many an Unsidhe warrior during battle. There were entire fields watered by the blood of my enemies. I try to gauge from his tone if he is angry. His voice is cool but not dangerous.

"I have been called that," I hesitantly agree. "My question is the same as before. I came with another. I would know of his condition."

The King frowns, darting his gaze to the nearest grimdelin.

Without prompting, the grimdelin drops to one knee, addressing the king. His voice is difficult to understand. It is clear that speaking is painful for him. "Found...in...cave. One faerie, one *auf*."

Auf... It's been so long since I've heard the old insult that I almost can't place it. That was what some of the older fae had called the Borrowed ones back when I was a child.

"And how is this auf now?" King Adalberon asks.

"In...mine...digging—" the grimdelin starts to answer.

"Idiot!" King Adalberon cuts him off, pressing his fingers to his forehead. "*How,* not where?"

I try to hide my smirk. Thanks to the grimdelin's weakness with language, I had gotten at least part of an answer to my next question. He is in a mine. What they are mining or where, I do not know yet, but even if I get no other answers, I am a step closer to finding him.

"Sorry...Majesty." The grimdelin cowers lower like he is expecting to be struck. Perhaps he is. The King does not strike me as someone who tolerates incompetence.

"Well?" King Adalberon asks after a second. "How is this auf?"

A second grimdelin, the one I took earlier as the superior, steps forward to answer when the first just shakes his head. "Alive, Majesty. Condition... otherwise...unknown. Not...habit...to worry. Always... plenty...of aufs."

Those words stir up my rage and it is all that I can do to stamp it down. I need to be in control now or risk losing the chance to get any answers.

King Adalberon turns to me. "Your...companion... is alive. I will send *Gar-lick* for a better assessment of his condition now." He waves to the still kneeling creature. *Gar-lick,* as he is apparently called, stumbles to his feet and backs out of the room. As soon as he is through the doors, I hear his speed pick up as he takes off running.

"So, Prince..." King Adalberon turns to me again, eyes narrowing. "Tell me. Why have you come to my kingdom?"

I think of the best way to word it. "My companion is seeking refuge from the Sidhe. I was escorting him to what I thought would be safety. Return him to me and we will leave your lands..." I swallow, convincing myself it is true before I add, "with no grudges held."

"I find myself wondering why a prince would take interest in the safety of a lowly auf. He must be truly special..." The King smirks. "Perhaps I should try him out for myself and s—"

Growling, I lunge for him, uncaring that I am both bound and unarmed. I would die—and likely *will* die— before I let him touch a hair on Rory's head. The King dodges my attack easily, sticking out his booted foot to kick me back onto the couch.

"Calm yourself, Prince. I have better toys to play with, I'm sure. But your reaction tells me what I want to know. He means something to you. He means *everything* to you." King Adalberon tilts his head. "Strange. A faerie with feelings..."

I tense, sensing the gears turning in his mind. I did not mean to reveal my feelings quite so obviously. Surely, he will use this against me.

There's no avoiding it now. I take the risk and ask what I really want to know. "What must I do for you to allow us to leave here in the condition we are now, or better?"

King Adalberon sits back, considering. "I have been looking to expand my territory. We have already started cultivating the Wilds but it will take...much time to untangle the magic that has twisted it. Give me the key to the Sidhe lands and I will release you both."

I know what he means by key. A chill spreads across my skin, unrelated to the cold we are sitting in. My mother is the steward of the Sidhe lands and I am her heir...Faerie will listen to none but us within our borders. If I were to pass my inheritance to another...like the King, for instance...

I would be removing our most sacred protection, more important even than the May-tree.

And for Rory...good gods, I know I'll do it.

Chapter Twenty-Three

King Adalberon

King Adalberon didn't think the young prince would agree to it. He fully anticipated the Sidhe brat to counter him with a promise of information or another, lesser, treason.

When the prince grits his teeth but nods, the King is honestly shocked. A thrill of excitement starts thrumming under his skin. Taming the Wilds would give the Unsidhe their first above-ground holdings. That meant sustainable food and room for his people to spread out—something they sorely need. Living ass to elbow like this, it's no surprise that his people are restless. Even with the arena fights every night, they are bored, quick to anger and quicker still to start trouble.

But the Sidhe lands? It is a prize he'd long since set aside as out of reach. Unattainable, until…it isn't.

"Unbind me and swear to release myself and my companion immediately and I will unlock the Sidhe lands for you," Prince Aries says, holding out his hands.

It is the best King Adalberon could have hoped for. With his vision earlier, he'd always intended on releasing the faerie. He may have even released the auf that was with him, just to be safe. No sense in leaving a reason for him to return. He'd told the prince what he hoped for to see what he'd counter with, able to do so because it wasn't a lie. He hadn't said that this was the *only* thing that would make him release the prince, after all.

"You have a deal."

Adalberon waits for the nearest grimdelin to unbind the prince, then pulls free his dagger and slices across his palm. Immediately, royal blue blood starts to bleed from the wound. Shifting his grip on it, he passes it, hilt first, to the young prince.

Aries barely pauses before he opens a similar wound on his own palm. Rather than pass the blade back, the prince drops it to the seat beside him. Adalberon frowns at the blood now staining his couch but doesn't protest. He'll summon one of the servants to clean it later.

He holds out his hand and the prince clasps it, their blood sealing the deal they'd just made. More than that, too—Adalberon feels the magic passing between them.

The keys to the Sidhe border, the power that will grant him access to Faerie beyond the borders of his kingdom…it is everything he'd ever hoped for and so much more. It fills him completely until his skin is singing with it and he feels almost drunk.

King Adalberon feels his end of the deal pulling at him though and knows he can't waste time relishing this. He stands, off balance, but steadies as he faces his grimdelins, the mole-like beasts he'd molded into the perfect underground guards. They would be no use to him in the Wilds or the Sidhe lands, but here their lack of sight is not a liability.

To the nearest, he orders, "Take the prince and his belongings to the East Gate. Make sure his companion joins him in exactly the condition he is in now."

The King plans to ride West with his army. The last thing he needs is the prince ahead of him spreading warning. Besides, if the prince manages to survive the lands to the east, he will have earned his life twice over.

* * * *

Rory

We've barely started working the next day — or after our rest, however long we had been allowed to sleep, it certainly hadn't felt like long enough — when a grimdelin hurries toward me. I tense, preparing myself to feel the bite of his whip on my back but instead, he grabs my arm, chattering at me too quickly for me to follow. Then, he starts dragging me away from my station.

"Hey!" I yelp, trying to pull free. God how I want to scratch him, watch him die quickly like the last one, but another would just take his place. Like rats, they are…too many of them to eradicate.

"You…come," he repeats himself slower. "King says…you go free…with Bloody Prince."

Bloody Prince…I have to imagine that's Aries, right? Had…had Aries negotiated for our freedom?

"But…what of the others?" I ask, planting my feet and forcing him to yank on my arm to budge me only a few inches. "I can't just…leave them here!"

I see the dead eyes, the mangled bodies. Many of them are so sick from the dust, they can barely stand, let alone be expected to keep up the unnatural pace the mole-men demand.

Death would be a mercy—and even that, Faerie apparently refuses to grant us.

Just as Faerie refuses to let us die from starvation or lack of water, she refuses to let the dust-sickness finish us off too. As I'd witnessed last night, it is left to us to send each other into the void when living becomes too much to bear.

I don't know if they'd meant to share that knowledge with me, but they'd had no choice after what I'd witnessed. Haylen, crouching at the bedside of a man who'd been partially crushed by falling rock. Initially, I'd thought he was providing medical care, or at the very least comfort.

Instead, Haylen had muttered what looked like a prayer before wrapping his big hands around man's fragile neck, strangling him. It had taken three men to hold me back while a fourth had frantically explained. The broken man would never heal enough to hold a hammer again and if he couldn't work, the grimdelins would punish him until he did.

Better to die quickly at the hands of one of their own than slowly beneath the mole-men's whips.

It is that thought that circles through my mind as the grimdelin shakes his head. "They stay. You go. Come. Now."

If I can't free them—and I can't, the changelings had explained all too well the many ways we were trapped here—then the least I can do is let them die quickly.

At the hands of a changeling.

At *my* hands. I stare down at my fingers as Angel surfaces inside me. He knows of the plan forming in my mind and together, we will the venom to coat our claws, thicker than it ever has before.

And as we pass the single well that all our water is drawn from, we let the venom spill down into it, poisoning it completely, for now and forever.

No changeling, no grimdelin or faerie, who drinks from this water will survive for long. How will they mine their ore now?

I hear the first body fall before they've closed the gate behind me for the final time.

Chapter Twenty-Four

Aries

The grimdelins bring Rory to me at the East Gate. I don't allow myself to relax until I see him, alive and in one piece. He is strangely red, like he is covered in dust, but he is walking on his own two feet and his jaw is set. If he is injured, I do not see evidence of it.

I rush toward him but as soon as my hands touch his skin, I scream, releasing him immediately.

Iron.

He is *covered* in iron dust and suddenly, I remember the grimdelin speaking of a mine. It seems I know now what he's been digging up. Now, the iron bars of the cages my fellow fae and I had been kept in make sense.

"Shit, you — you can't touch me yet," Rory stutters. At first, I think it from fear, then I realize how bitterly cold it is. We are standing in a cave on the opposite side of the mountain from where we were first grabbed and outside, it is storming. Pellets of hail strike the stone near the cave's mouth. The wind is screaming.

Rory is still barefoot.

But he is here, and he is alive, and we are free to leave.

Or at least, we should be, but I hear what sounds like the King roar with anger in the tunnel. "I want him flayed! His skin stretched into a canvas! I want to paint with his blood! *I want to wear his teeth as a bracelet!*"

Rory, beneath the layer of iron dust, goes pale. "We should go. We should go *now*."

I want to ask what he did—because in between all the threats, I hear the King cursing the "human brat" and "mortal bastard", and I doubt there's another changeling capable of inspiring such anger in another as mine is—but as the voice grows closer, I decide he's right.

"Come, quick," I urge him, running toward the mouth of the cave. I suddenly see the flaw in my deal with the King. He was to release us immediately, with all our belongings and in the same condition we currently were—but there is nothing to prevent him from recapturing us again and torturing us *after* he releases us.

Thankfully, I'd taken the time spent waiting for Rory's arrival to tie a rope to one of the sturdier looking stalagmites to ease our journey down the nearly flat mountain side to the ledge twenty feet below us. It is hard to see through the blizzard raging outside but I can just make out the start of a path leading down from it.

The poor visibility should help hide us from sight, even if it makes the journey more miserable.

Rory doesn't waste time. He grabs the rope and practically flings himself out the mouth of the tunnel, descending it quickly. I follow him. I start to lower myself just as the King bursts into the cave. His giant shoulders are heaving, his face tomato-red with anger.

We lock eyes for just a second before I let myself drop, gripping the rope tight as I slide down. "Quick, there's a path," Rory says as soon as my feet hit the ledge and I follow him at a run. It is narrow and treacherous, but nowhere near as steep as the one we'd taken up the other side of the mountain.

I look back only once. If we are being followed, I don't see anyone.

King Adalberon

The Bloody Prince and his surprisingly murderous changeling escape King Adalberon's clutches by mere seconds. Considering the deal he'd made — and the prophecy that Faerie had shown to him — it is likely for the best. Oh, but how he would love to get his hands on them again, show them what *real* torture feels like.

He can't believe that an auf — an *auf*, of all things! — had managed to single-handedly put down his entire stock of chattel. His convenient source of manual labor, taken out in one day. If it weren't for the army he'd already massed at the West Gate, he'd hunt the pair down and make them pay for it. Today, they could consider themselves lucky.

King Adalberon sighs, watching the pair disappear into the falling snow. He has no idea how the auf had done it — poison, perhaps? His grimdelins were not the brightest, they could have missed it in their search of him — but he doubts it will happen again. Once he secures the Sidhe lands for his own, he can replenish his chattel again.

And with that much land at his disposal, he will no longer need to clear the lower pits of iron to house his population anyway. Cheered by that realization, King Adalberon turns his back on the two fleeing men and rejoins his army.

Chapter Twenty-Five

Aries

We don't stop running until we reach the base of the mountain. Going down proves much easier than climbing had been, at least. Everything in me screams for me to pick up Rory, who is clearly exhausted and in pain, but until we have a way to wash the iron dust from his skin, I can't touch him, not even to help him up. Already my hands are blistered from when I grabbed him in the cave. If I need to fight, I'll be at a disadvantage.

While the Unsidhe King hasn't sent anyone after us yet — or if he has, I've seen no signs of them — he could still change his mind, and that's not accounting for whatever beasts or monsters we may run into out here. The land beyond the Unsidhe Court is a mystery to me. We have no maps of it, nor have any rumors made their way to my ears.

Thankfully, the land seems, so far, devoid of life. We reach the banks of a river and though I know it's a risk, I break the icy surface with my sword. Reluctantly, we both drink from it before Rory strips from his clothes and submerges himself in it. His skin is tinged with blue after mere seconds and he quickly swipes at the now muddy dust, jaw chattering.

I wish we could have waited until we found someplace warm but without knowing how long that will take, we can't risk it. Because of the iron, I've had to stay at least two arms' lengths away from him this entire time and even that far, I can feel my lungs burning from the exposure to the iron. I need to be able to stay closer to him in case we are attacked.

As soon as he emerges, frozen but iron free, from the river, I envelop him in the thick cloak the Unsidhe had thankfully returned to us with our belongings. I rub him dry without speaking. What can I possibly say?

He redresses in the last of my spare shirts and a pair of my pants. They pool over his feet and I have to cut a stretch of rope to use as a belt to keep them around his waist. Then, we keep moving.

We need shelter. I try instinctively to ask Faerie for help but she is silent. If she hears me, she doesn't answer.

I don't blame her.

I can't allow myself to think of what I've done, not until we are somewhere safe.

Rory spots it first. "There! What is that?" He points off to the right, toward what I'd thought was yet another column of spinning snow. Between the blowing snow and frost coated boulders, all I can see is white.

I tilt my head, squinting. It looks like… "Steam?" I suggest. If I'm right, that means that somewhere over there is something hot. A spring, perhaps? Whatever it is, it's likely our best shot at this point.

We angle toward it.

By the time we reach it, both of us are shaking too hard to speak to each other. I can't imagine how much pain Rory must be in. His feet, the little I can see of them, are waxy. If they aren't frostbitten already, they will be soon.

As soon as we reach the edge of the small hot spring, Rory strips out of his clothing and walks right into the water. I follow close on his heels. At this point, it's so cold that I don't care what critters might be lurking below the glittering surface. The heat is calling me.

"Oh fuck," Rory says, sinking immediately down until the water reaches his chin. I do the same, cursing as well. It is painfully hot. I can tell that it feels warmer than it is, though. It is not, as I initially fear, hot enough to do damage.

"I'm never getting out," Rory says as he wades deeper into the spring. It's not overly large but it is just the right depth to keep us immersed. My skin starts to sting as blood returns to chilled extremities. It reminds me to check Rory over.

"Let me see your feet," I say as I swim to him.

"Kinky," Rory teases, but he floats onto his back, bringing his feet closer to the surface. I carefully take each of them in my hands, bringing them close enough I can see his skin through the water without accidentally lifting them free of it.

They are no longer waxy. Instead, they are almost cherry red. He whimpers as I massage them. I glance up at his face to see him biting his lip. "I don't think you'll lose them," I say, and I'm fairly confident in my assessment. Somehow, by some miracle, they are not the blue-black I'd feared. The fact that he is feeling pain in them is a good sign.

"Aries," Rory says, floating closer once I release him. "What are we supposed to do now? I might have teased about staying in here forever, but we have to get out eventually."

I know he's right. Unfortunately, I don't have an answer. Not long term, and not short term either. As soon as we climb out of the water, we'll freeze. It had felt warmer on the banks of the spring, but not warm enough to stand around, dripping wet, for any length of time.

And even if we manage to dress and somehow find a way to dry, then what? We can't go back to the Sidhe, not now that I've handed it over to the Unsidhe, and clearly we aren't welcome back in the Court Under the Mountain. The Wilds aren't an option either. We'd been lucky to survive the Wilds the first time through.

Suddenly, a beam of light strikes the water between us and, for the first time since we entered the Unsidhe Court, I hear Faerie's voice speaking to me.

She is as angry as I have ever heard her, but despite her anger…it seems she has decided not to abandon me.

"Go. Leave this place you no longer wish to call home, and do not come back. I will not welcome you again, Prince of Nothing."

The light starts to harden, then splits open—a tear to Earth. I meet Rory's eyes, then smile. "Let's go home."

He takes my hand when I offer it and together, we swim through.

Chapter Twenty-Six

King Adalberon

King Adalberon did not find what he expected to find when he brought his army across the Wilds and into the Sidhe lands. Despite that, he can't say he's disappointed. There has been no resistance as he's laid claim to acre after acre of land. The few Sidhe fae who tried to fight were easily overcome.

Where is the Queen's army? he wonders with every slave they capture.

And for every furlong of land they claim, his curiosity grows. There is something wrong here. Too many unnatural things to be explained away — from the fields of flowers with their gnashing teeth to the salt-poisoned streams.

His hopes of easily tillable fields and settleable homes are quickly dashed. No wonder the young prince had been so quick to sell out his Court. It is dying anyway.

Still, he continues on and they make it to the heart of the Sidhe lands uncontested. He is cautious as he approaches the Queen's Castle, certain that *here* at least he will face resistance.

But the castle is gone. All that is left is a maw-like gash in the earth, deep and wide, and nearby, the tumbled remains of what, if his memory serves, used to be a stable.

"Round up the survivors," he orders his men. He can see several along the edge of the ravine, covered in dirt with vacant eyes, but there are surely more. No point in letting them go to waste here.

Queen Nuala may not have recognized the signs of rot in her kingdom until it was too late, but he is far older and wiser than her. She might not remember how the Wilds came to be, but he does. After all, unlike her, he had been fully grown when the Autumn Court fell. He still remembers watching their land grow strange and twisted by the day.

Sometimes, when he lets himself get too tired, he can still see the horrid things the unbound magic had turned the Autumn faeries into. He has no sympathy for the Sidhe bastards, but none have ever called him wasteful. Those who still live will be taken back with him to be put to use.

Adalberon nudges his steed, a giant boar he'd caught with his own hands, closer to the ravine, staring down into the shattered earth with a frown. How had this happened? Unsidhe scholars have many theories of what broke the Autumn Court but few of them are willing to agree on any one of them. Some claim that the Autumn King had turned his back on Faerie and Faerie had retaliated. A few argue that it was a Sidhe curse.

There isn't enough evidence to support any theory and to date he has largely considered the studies to be a waste of time. It takes valuable resources — food, camping gear, guards — to send the expeditions into the Wilds to gather evidence. Resources he's long believed to be better spent elsewhere.

Now, with the quickly approaching death of the Spring Court, he wonders if he'll regret his reticence.

There is nothing he can do for it now. Making a note to himself to send out at least a few teams when he gets home, he turns from the ravine, staring instead at the rubble of what used to be the stables. Perhaps some of the steeds have survived. The Sidhe horses are not only fast and hardy, but in lean times provide enough meat to fill the bellies of three men. They are well worth the amount of grain required to care for them.

Adalberon dismounts from his own steed, knowing that the boar will scare away any horses that remain. Taking a few coils of rope with him, in case he finds one, he approaches the toppled ruins from the side. Before he can round the corner, however, he hears movement in the grass.

Placing his hand on the hilt of his sword, he moves slowly toward it.

He finds, not a horse or beast, but a faerie man struggling to his knees. Silver-haired and slender, with a sharpness in his eyes that King Adalberon finds…intriguing. *Has always*, he admits if only to himself, *found intriguing*, for he recognizes this faerie.

This is the Queen's left hand. How many meetings had Adalberon sat through with Nuala, trying to ignore this self-same faerie? Her stern-faced shadow…

And now here he is, on his knees and already beautifully broken just for him. From his vantage point,

Adalberon can see the fresh amputation of the faerie's lower leg.

Anik, his name was, then Merrit, and now Marik. The faerie spots him and stiffens, recognition flooding his icy eyes. He reaches for his bloody dagger but Adalberon, uninjured and standing, moves quicker. He kicks the faerie hard in his chest, sending him sprawling back.

"Well, well, well...what do we have here?" King Adalberon purrs down at him.

"How is this possible?" Marik asks, his horror easy to hear.

Adalberon laughs. "It was only a matter of time." With the condition of the Sidhe lands as they are now, he knows it's the truth. Even if the prince hadn't sold it out for the life of a silly mortal boy, he would have made it here eventually. He can feel the magic that would have denied him entry guttering out.

But perhaps he had not made out so poorly in the bargain after all. If he'd waited, he would not be here now, standing over the arrogant faerie warrior he'd spent many a night dreaming of.

Now, wherever Queen Nuala is, she cannot stop him from taking her shadow and making him his pet. He grabs for a coil of rope.

Marik puts up a hell of a fight for a man who has clearly just amputated his own leg. By the time Adalberon has him hogtied and over his shoulder, he's even broken a sweat, something that hasn't happened in ages.

"I admire your spirit, Pet. I hope you don't let me break it too quickly."

Whistling, he carries the still-struggling faerie to his boar, tossing him, still bound, across the broad shoulders. He swings up behind him, then grabs hold of the waistband of the faerie's trousers just above the curve of his ass to hold him in place.

"Grab what you can," King Adalberon calls to his men. "Leave the rest. It's time to go home."

Chapter Twenty-Seven

Rory

Our cottage is quaint. There are two bedrooms — the largest, Aries and I share, and I've taken over the smaller as my art studio — and only one bathroom. It does, however, have indoor plumbing. That was something I'd insisted on, along with an open concept kitchen and living room.

Between the money Aries had saved from his job at the Bureau and the trinkets I'd...found...during my time prowling the streets, we could have bought something bigger, but as soon as I'd laid eyes on this one, I'd known it was the one.

It looks so much like the cottage Aries used to have in Faerie. For all the terrible things I had suffered across the veil, there'd been good things too, memories I no longer feel the need to lock away in murals.

Now, the only paintings I make are the ones that hang in museums across the provinces. Who would have thought people would pay thousands of dollars for the art I was making as part of my court-ordered therapy sessions? There is a high demand for my twisted faerie tale aesthetic.

I'd been nervous when Aries and I jumped through the tear that had opened in the hot spring six weeks ago. More like terrified, actually—there was no telling how much time had passed on Earth while we'd been in Faerie.

Apparently, just enough for the Blanks to make some improvements.

They'd hired Watchers—wixes with the gift of foresight—to predict when and where unauthorized tears would open. That meant that when Aries and I had spilled through—completely naked—into lake Michigan, only a dozen feet away from Navy Pier, there were several heavily armed BAA agents waiting to arrest us.

Thankfully, it was the most polite arrest I've ever been subjected to. The agents on the pier had quickly scrounged up some spare clothes for us to dress in first before escorting us, not to a jail cell, where the iron would have made Aries sick, but to an intake center.

Apparently, these were *not* new. They were just unique to the State of Illinois. It was one of the few governments in the entire Federation that had updated their civil rights legislation to include protections for Elyries.

At the intake center, Aries and I had been forced to sit through a lesson on not only the history of Earth but the various laws and regulations we'd be expected to follow. Thankfully, one of the staff members had apparently worked in the Old York office prior to the Blood Storm. He was quite a bit older now thanks to the time difference between our two worlds, but he'd still recognized Aries.

In exchange for Aries agreeing to come back to work for the Bureau—with the condition that he never works past sunset, due to his newly discovered knowledge of my fear of the dark, and that he'd get at least one weekend off each month—he'd helped streamline Aries' visa application. Once his residency card had come through, we'd been allowed to leave. Conditionally, of course. Our caseworker had pulled out a book of houses available to rent or purchase. We'd narrowed it down to three—this cottage tucked along the Glenview Riverwalk, an apartment in Marina City, or a colonial in one of the suburbs. As soon as we saw this one, I'd fallen in love.

We'd signed the paperwork, then I'd been placed under house arrest while my asylum case gets processed. My paperwork is taking a bit longer than my caseworker expected, and he'd had to loop in a lawyer. I am not human enough to claim citizenship, especially since I can't tell them where—or when—I was born. But I am also, it seems, not fae enough to comply with the treaty made between the human government and the Sidhe. My lawyer promised that there is nothing to worry about.

She says that my case is hung up on a technicality. Once they decide what species to classify me as—they are leaning toward a lesser demon—they will be able to bring it before the judge. The label is no more accurate than any of the other options, but the doctor who'd examined Angel said that the resemblance is close enough.

I don't care what they decide to call me.

I'm not even all that worried about how long it will take them to finish my paperwork, as long as they don't try to send me back. I'm in no hurry to wander around the city, no matter that both Aries and my lawyer have promised me that it's nothing like Old York was.

Besides, it's not like I have any need to leave.

My therapist meets me here when she needs to see me. We take tea on the back porch sometimes. Other days, she watches me paint.

Food, I'd discovered quickly, can be delivered right to our doorstep, as can clothing.

Everything I need is in these four walls.

Except, at the moment, Aries.

I put down my paintbrush and leave my studio, wandering to the front door. I open it, but don't cross the threshold. I have a few feet leeway onto the porch before the monitor clasped around my ankle will start beeping. I don't push it that close. No matter that they've promised it will send a warning first, I am terrified that someone will learn I've stepped too far out and I'll be ripped away from Aries and our home here and sent back to Faerie to rot.

I won't risk it.

I stare at the slab of pavement where Aries parks his motorcycle.

Empty.

I glare at it, slipping my hand in my pocket to pull out the cellphone my attorney had dropped off for me. There are only three names in the contact list. Jared Ackles, my lawyer, Noel Dungey, my therapist, and Aries.

I slam my thumb down on Aries name, then lift it to my ear. It rings twice before he answers it. "Rory? Everything okay?"

"You're not home yet," I tell him, pouting. "The sun is setting, and you're not here."

"It's not even five yet, sweet hart," he points out.

I don't care about his logic, or…or his ability to read an analog clock, something I still haven't quite mastered.

"The sun. Is setting. And you. Are. Not. Here." I emphasize each word, glaring so hard at the pavement that if I could, I would set it on fire with my mind.

"I'm leaving now, I just have to lock up my gun," Aries promises.

And since he can't lie, I know he means it. Still, I sniff. "Will you bring home lasagna? But not that kind from Luigi's, I want Mario's. The good stuff. With the cheese, you know the one."

"Yes, deer." Aries sounds like he's laughing, but I know he's not. He knows better than to laugh at me.

"Are you laughing?" I ask. This time, I hear him snicker.

"Would I laugh at you?"

Now I know that he's laughing, because if he wasn't, he would have told me. Whenever he answers my question with a question, I know it's because his answer would have been a lie.

"It's not my fault you're late." Still clutching the phone, I sink down to my butt in the doorway to wait. I never used to be this clingy. My therapist promises that it is just a phase that will pass.

And she'd better fucking be right, because I hate feeling this needy. I used to be able to spend weeks roaming Old York on my own, never needing to see another living person that I wasn't pickpocketing. Now, I can barely go eight hours without worrying that he's gotten bored of me and left.

Fucking trauma.
Fucking PTSD.
Fucking faeries.
Yeah, I decide.
Fucking faeries.

Aries

I had already placed an order with Mario's before Rory called, anticipating from the seventeen texts he'd sent me since I left this morning that today was one of his rough ones. He still hasn't told me everything he went through in Faerie—not the first time and not the last one either. We speak of some things during our joint sessions, but he isn't willing to share everything with me.

I am trying not to press. My own therapist, a human named Finn, has reminded me a half-dozen times to have patience. Rory will share what he needs to when he's ready, *if* he's ready.

And if he never is, I need to accept that.

I know I am responsible for much of the pain Rory carries, directly or indirectly. How much of the trauma he holds is from the tortures he'd experienced at my very hand? I may never know.

And that is my burden to carry.

I lock up my gun and push away from my desk. I pause at my supervisor's desk just long enough to say, "I have to leave." She waves me away. I'd warned her this morning that Rory had a therapy session this morning and I might need to leave early. Thankfully, the Chicago branch of the Bureau is a much better assignment than the York one was, and she'd been understanding.

It's amazing what a difference accepting the Elyries instead of othering them has. The crime rates are the lowest in the federation and the economy is one of the strongest. Even unemployment is low — directly contradicting one of York's biggest arguments favoring their segregationist policies.

Some of the jobs that the humans hate the most are perfectly suited for certain Elyries. Brownies are perfect housekeepers, and the golguthra — who feast on trash and refuse — are highly efficient garbagemen. Of course there had to be *some* regulations — even the vampires agreed that they should not be permitted to be phlebotomists, but by and large, my job seems easy and the city safe.

If it weren't for traffic, it would be absolutely perfect.

Fingers tapping on the handles of my bike, I wait impatiently for the carriage in front of me to make its way through the intersection. Not for the first time, I wish I hadn't been forced to leave Ayna behind. I hope he is enjoying Faerie. I hope he is safe.

I can feel that he is alive — the bridle still bound to me would have dissolved otherwise — but that is it.

Getting around the city would be easier on a horse. My bike is too unwieldy at the slow speeds I'm forced to drive it and, unlike in York, I'm required to yield to literally everything else on the road. Maybe I should sell it and buy a horse. One of my coworkers spoke highly of a stable near Lincoln Park.

Or maybe I should just get a bicycle, I think as I watch a bike messenger peel around the corner in front of me, pulling a little three-wheeled wagon behind him. *It would certainly be easier to bring home the lasagna.*

When I finally get back to our cottage, I spot Rory waiting for me.

He is sitting, knees to his chest, in the open doorway, his bare toes almost touching the wood of the front porch. I can't help but smile at his mulish expression as I carefully pull the two mini-containers of lasagna out from my saddlebags. It would be cheaper to get one pan but, as I'd learned the first time, the aluminum tray was too big to fit in the saddlebags. I'd had to balance it on my lap and cling to it the whole way home. Not only had I burned my thighs and dick, but I'd nearly lost it more than twice.

Another reason to lose the motorcycle.

Carrying them up the porch, I stop in front of Rory and smile. "Going to let me in, deer?"

"Only because you brought food," he grumbles, sliding over just enough for me to squeeze by.

I know he's not really mad at me. His therapy sessions always leave him in one of two moods — clingy and pissed off, or morose and distant. Honestly, I prefer his anger. It burns hotter but fades quicker.

I carry the lasagna into the kitchen. By the time I'm setting it on the counter, I hear him close the door and his footsteps padding over the tile. *He didn't slam it this time,* I tell myself.

"Did you even miss me?" Rory asks, and though he sounds irritated, I can hear the fear beneath the anger.

I spin immediately, curling my fingers around his waist and tugging him to me. Since coming back to Earth, whatever had been blocking my glamour had disappeared. I've taken my favorite form again, taller and broader than him, my antlers put away. His head barely comes to my chest.

He clings to me, gripping my uniform jacket tightly with his fingers. "Of course I missed you, sweet hart," I promise him, holding him even tighter. Honestly, the only reason I still go to work is because Rory's therapist insists that he needs to spend some time on his own.

She is worried that he is "too codependent". Personally, I'd stitch his body to mine if I could get away with it. From the time I leave the house in the morning, all I can think of is coming home to him.

"I hate your job. You only work because you want to get away from me, I know it." Rory finally loosens his fingers, trying to step back but I don't let him. I'm fully aware that he doesn't mean it but if he needs to hear me say it, then I'll tell him a thousand times.

"I would happily stay home with you all the time if I could," I promise. "Give me a kiss?"

He sticks out his lower lip, glaring at me for so long I worry he won't, then he finally sighs. "Fine. But try to get home on time tomorrow."

I don't bother to point out that I'm actually home an hour early. It won't help his anger and I know exactly how he feels. "Yes, love," I promise him instead. It's an easy vow to make — nothing short of death could make me purposefully stay away from him any longer than I need to for his health.

And mine, I force myself to admit. I'm nearly as codependent as he is.

He sticks to my side as I scoop up our meals, only stepping away when we get to the table. Even then, he scooches his chair closer to mine. Knowing that, despite all the hell I put him through, he still craves to be close to me is the best feeling ever.

This is not the life I expected to have. I'd always assumed that someday, I'd return to Faerie and take my place as King. I hadn't wanted to. I'd planned to push it off as long as I could, but it was always there in the back of my mind, where I would eventually end up.

That dream — or nightmare, really — is officially dead now.

Instead, I have a new dream — a dream of waking up with Rory every morning and falling asleep in his arms every night. I have not seen Angel much, but sometimes he comes out just to visit. He does not like the smell of Rory's paint but he loves listening to me read to him.

Maybe Rory has developed a fear of leaving the house and a strong distaste for the smell of mint. Maybe Rory still has nightmares, and maybe I still struggle to fall asleep, terrified he will disappear if I close my eyes.

Maybe this isn't the life I expected…

But maybe, it's everything I could have dreamed of, if I'd had the courage to look beyond the expectations of my birthright.

Maybe, it's perfect.

Chapter Twenty-Eight

Rory

"I'll make the popcorn. It's your turn to pick a movie," I tell Aries after dinner, finally feeling calm enough to leave his side, even if it's only for a few minutes. Two minutes and forty-five seconds, to be precise. I carry the steaming bag to the couch and drop it onto Aries' lap, shaking my fingers to alleviate the sting.

"Ouch! Goddamnit, Rory!" Aries snaps, leaping to his feet and brushing off his dick. He's smiling though, so I grin and plop down in his seat. He grumbles but moves to the other half of the loveseat.

I snag the popcorn bag off the floor and carefully open it, digging out a handful before I tip it toward him. "It's unsalted," I promise. No one would ever convince me it tastes better this way, but it's starting to grow on me.

Aries snags a few kernels, then stretches across me to reach the remote. He turns on the holo screen. "One of my coworkers said the new Kaelith Lux movie is good."

Kaelith Lux is one of the few non-humans who'd made it to the silver screen. Maybe it was due to his good looks—the ankhuban certainly upstaged every one of his coworkers. Aries and I have been working our way through his backlist over the past few weeks. Neither one of us had spent much time watching movies before. He'd been too busy with work and I'd been too preoccupied with staying out of jail and out of sight.

"Is this the one where he's planning a heist? Or the one where he's dying and needs to make amends with his estranged lover?" I ask, trying to remember which one just came out and which one was coming out next month.

"Definitely the heist one," Aries answers. He looks apologetic when he meets my gaze and adds, "I'm not sure I'll be able to sit through the other one."

"That's good, because I wasn't looking forward to trying not to cry through the whole thing anyway." I keep my voice upbeat but grab his hand and tug him closer. "Scooch over, you're too far away. And start the movie, won't you?"

We're both, I know, suffering from trauma, just of different kinds. The big difference is that I'm dealing with mine. Not well, and not quickly, but I talk to my therapist and, for the most part, try to take her advice when I can. The only thing I've refused to do is leave the cottage. But when I get stuck in memories, I paint them on canvas. When the dark gets too overwhelming, I turn on the lights and practice my breathing. When I worry that Aries is going to leave me, I write it in my journal and leave it out for Aries to read.

Aries refuses to deal with the loss of his old lovers.

It's like he thinks that if he ignores the pain long enough, it will go away. Honestly, I think he feels that acknowledging the pain of their deaths is in some way a betrayal of me. My therapist tells me I need to give him time, that he'll talk about it when he's ready.

I decide now that I'll give him a week, and if he isn't ready to talk about it by then, I'll tie him down and make him.

Aries starts the movie.

It's not as funny as I expect it to be but it is definitely steamy. When Kaelith's character gets fucked — in the shower, behind artfully frosted glass — by the federal agent meant to be arresting him, I have to readjust myself in my pants. I look at Aries and he is clearly as turned on as I am. His pupils are blown and fist is clenched on his thigh.

Not bothering to pause the movie — it's almost over anyway — I toss aside the nearly empty popcorn bag and straddle Aries' lap. I run my fingers through his hair, tipping his head back to meet his eyes. It's easier without his antlers in the way, but I do miss the easy handholds sometimes.

"Want some help with that?" I ask, grinding my ass against his dick.

Groaning, he grabs my hips and holds me still. "Fuck, yes," he says, "but I had something a little different in mind tonight." There's something in his voice, a tension that wasn't there before, and I'm curious.

"Oh?"

"I want *this*," Aries says, and now it's my turn to moan when he lets go of my hip to cup my erection instead, "inside me tonight."

"You want me to top?" I freeze, surprised. Except for that one time at the loch, he's never hinted again that he'd want that. And even then, he'd been playing with Angel, not me. Maybe that's what he meant? "Do you want me to ask Angel?"

Aries frowns, sitting up slightly and shifting me further down his thighs. "If that's what you and he both want. But *only* if it's what you both want."

Angel starts to stir, clearly realizing we're talking about him.

"What's going on?" he asks me. He's been quiet the past few weeks. He'd promised me he wasn't going anywhere, that he was just taking everything in and processing.

Processing what, he hadn't said.

I explain Aries' request.

"*It's up to you,*" Angel promises. *"If you want to be alone with him, I can go back to sleep."*

"No!" I answer, suddenly terrified at the thought of doing this on my own.

Aries must realize that I'm talking it over with Angel because he sits quietly, ever patient, and waits.

"You want me to stay?" Angel asks.

"*I want to do this together.*" And not just because it will be my first time ever topping and I trust him to walk me through it—not that he's ever topped, but clearly, he's *much* more dominant than I am, he'd proved that at the loch. I've sensed his feelings for Aries growing, felt his curiosity as the two of us had made love.

It feels right that he would be a part of this. Now that I know we can both be present without either one of us endangering the other, there's no reason to keep him stuck asleep all the time. Not only has his feelings for Aries been growing, but I sense my own feelings toward Angel have been changing as well.

He no longer feels like a scary stranger in my body.

He feels like my partner.

I know he can hear all these thoughts running through my mind and I feel his consciousness blushing, or whatever the equivalent of it is for him. Heat fills my chest.

Slowly, he surfaces. Not all the way, not enough to push me down, just enough that I feel our fingers lengthen and our claws grow sharper.

"We have decided," Angel says, grinning at Aries. "Do you think you can handle us both?"

"My loves," Aries promises, "I will handle whatever you are willing to give me. Take me. I'm yours."

* * * *

Angel

I wait until I feel Aries finally give in to sleep beside me before I open Rory's eyes. Like our lover, he is asleep as well. After we'd claimed our Princeling together, we'd had a nice long talk, just the two of us. He'd given me permission to stay. He'd even given me permission to use his — our — body when I wish, so long as I don't do anything crazy.

I am not sure what he thinks would be crazy, but since I have no intention of doing anything that would bring harm to our body, I'd agreed. This will be the first time, outside of those when he was in danger, that I can explore.

Quietly, I slip from the bed, padding through the house on our — *my* — bare feet. The back door creaks when I open it, but I hear nothing from the bedroom. The hardest part for Aries seems to be falling to sleep. Once he's managed it, he doesn't wake easily. Inside me, Rory stirs but only for a moment.

I don't step outside. The collar around our ankle keeps us from going too far, but I don't need to go anywhere. I've seen him watching us. He will find me.

I leave the door open and walk back into the kitchen, pulling out a loaf of stale bread. By the time I've torn it into pieces, he is here. I pucker my lips toward the bird. The raven flutters his wings as he cautiously hops along the counter. He stays just out of reach. I carefully toss him a piece of bread.

Slowly, I feed him. When it is gone, the raven cocks his head at me. He croaks, then flies out through the open door. I follow him to the threshold, watching him soar up through the dark trees and into the night.

In the morning, Rory finds a single gold earring on the welcome mat.

He doesn't know where it comes from, though he gushes over it to Aries on the phone, but I know it is a trinket from my new friend. Soon, he will trust me enough to speak to me. Ravens are messengers, capable of crossing the boundaries between worlds. Aries may believe that we are safe here, Rory may believe that this cottage will protect him...but I will not be tricked. Now that Rory and Aries have accepted me, now that they have shown me what it is like to feel, I will not risk losing them.

Just because Faerie sent us back, doesn't mean she is done with us.

If she starts making plans, I will know of it.

I will be the watcher in the night and the keeper of ravens. I will be whatever I need to be to keep Aries and Rory safe, whether they know of it or not.

Sign up for our newsletter and find out about all our romance book releases, eBook sales and promotions, sneak peeks and FREE romance books!

Want to see more from this author? Here's a taster for you to enjoy!

Demon Daddy:
The Faerie King's Prisoner
KD Ellis

Excerpt

Nyx

In the Court Under the Mountain, it is dark and quiet. Even the sticky spiral cobweb that stretches from dozens of anchor points along the cave wall is still. With most of the Court on an expedition to overtake the Sidhe lands, my spider friend has taken the opportunity to do some exploring of her own.

Maybe I should follow in her footsteps.

I slip off my cot and pad my way to the opening of the little cave I've claimed as my own while the King is away. It is too small for my humanoid form — I'd have a hard time squeezing my head in without crimping my ears, let alone the rest of me — but is just right for me like this.

I know that I am small for a *cait-sith*. Barely the size of a common house cat, if I'm brutally honest with myself. It's how I ended up here in the first place. No point wasting precious food on the runt of the litter, not when there were six other mouths to feed. My parents had gifted me to the King before I'd opened my eyes. I'd never seen them, wouldn't recognize them if they stood right in front of me.

Instead, I'd grown up here in the Court, raised by an old *cu-sith* couple who'd never managed to have pups of their own, until I was old enough to be of some use. First as a page, running missives for the King and tidying his bedchamber, then as a scribe as well, once I'd learned my letters. Then, when my voice started to break, I'd joined my King in his bed. It was only recently that I'd been granted the honor of being the King's Voice, his herald in the Court.

But with the King gone, and most of his Court with him, for the first time since I was a kitten, I find myself with no assignments and no demands on my time. I know exactly how I plan to fill it.

I don't bother shifting. Instead, I pad on four paws to the great kitchen. It is large and, even with most of the Court gone, bustling with activity. I slip around ankles and dodge unwary feet, making my way to the back wall. Already, I can feel the heat wafting off the bread oven.

The cook would notice me at the front or side, but there's just enough of a gap between the back of the brick oven and the cave wall for me to slip behind it. It's hotter back here, almost too hot, but I bask in it.

Heat is a precious thing here in the Winter Court.

It never lasts long enough.

The cook finds me eventually, chasing me out with a straw-bristle broom, screaming about vermin as he sweeps out after me, but I am too fast for him.

Vermin, he says! I resolve to shit in his shoes later.

I pad down the hall. Before I make it back to my little cave, I freeze. There! It's beautiful and everything in me tells me I need it, even if rationally, I know I can't. The ice-refracted light glimmers on the dark stone, tempting as diamonds. I crouch, butt in the air and tail flicking back and forth. One good pounce, that's all I need…

Keeping my eyes locked on the glimmer, I wait for the perfect moment, then pounce. My paws land on the sparkles and hold it in place. A bit of kneading later, and my claws have worked the light free from the stone. It lies, solid and warm, like a glowing coal.

Purring, I pick it up carefully in my mouth and carry it with me to my cave.

I can't wait to show the King.

* * * *

Marik

Shit and sweat and underneath both, the sharp stench of urine. I reek of it, from my snarled, matted hair to my dusty clothes. It clings to my skin and when I breathe, I can taste it. Of course, that could be from trying to bite the boar in hopes he'd buck us off and I'd somehow be able to work my bonds free.

It hadn't worked.

All I'd ended up with was a mouthful of hair and the sound of the Unsidhe King laughing behind me.

Dusk falls and both dawns rise, and still we are riding. The King's grip on the back of my pants has never wavered and no matter how I struggle, I can't loosen my ropes. They bite at my skin, and whatever they are made of makes my skin itch like I just rolled around in a spread of leadwort.

I am not bothered by the discomfort—I've certainly had much worse. It is the indignity that stings. To be caught like a rabbit in a snare and trussed up like dinner, all without laying a single finger on my opponent? If I had my sword, I might fall on it from the shame.

The day grows warm. I can feel the sun burning my skin, sucking the moisture from it like desert sand, and thoughts of escaping start to fade. Perhaps a chance will reveal itself later, perhaps not, but without water, I won't be strong enough to seize the opportunity.

Eventually, though, a calm settles. As I lie over the heaving shoulders of the boar, I realize that in the long run, not much has changed. Prisoner of our crazy Queen or of this unknown King, what difference could there be? Surely, there are no new ways I can be tortured, no new pains to endure.

Once I decide to accept, at least for now, my predicament, I feel my muscles stop straining. The boar's gait is easier to endure, his steps no longer painfully jarring. He still stinks.

With my mind less occupied, though, there is nothing to distract me from the feeling of the King's hand at my back. It is large, but unlike those of the summer fae I am used to, his skin is cool where it touches mine. I feel the urge to press against it, let it cool my heated flesh, and it takes the little energy I have left to resist.

I force myself to concentrate on the throbbing emptiness at the end of my leg instead. The reminder of what I've lost immediately jolts me like lightning. Always, I have measured my worth in the reach of my blade and the surety of my footwork. Even the Queen, for all that she used my body as her personal sex toy, kept me at her side first and foremost because of my skills as a warrior.

She would have no use for me now.

If she's even alive… Could she have survived the crack in the ground? Would the walls of her castle have crushed her, or had Faerie spared her? Straining my neck to look at the land around us, I am no longer sure. Things are changing, twisting in new and horrid ways. A shiver creeps down my spine when I see a dead fawn, its body tangled up in creeper vines.

"It will only get worse." King Adalberon's voice suddenly breaks the silence and I startle, then burn with shame at betraying my old mentor's earliest teachings. *Never let them see your fear.*

"Why?" I force myself to ask, curiosity overcoming my sullen urge to remain silent. "What's happening?"

"Your Court is dying, just like the Autumn Court did." He says it calmly, as if the thought of a Court dying wasn't terrifying. I'd always wondered why there were three Courts but four seasons...always wondered what happened to Autumn.

"Why?" I ask again. Is this because of the Queen's experiments, or something else? Is all of Faerie destined to die someday?

King Adalberon laughs. "Why? Why?" he mocks me. "You sound just like a query-bird."

Fire burns in my chest and I fight the urge to try to strike him. Between the bindings and my position, rump up over the back of the boar, I know it would be pointless, but fuck how I want to try anyway.

"Excuse me for being curious why my entire Court is turning into a...a..." I don't even know what to call it and stumble on my words, but what I do get out is dripping with ire.

"I'll allow you your curiosity for now, pet, because it amuses me. But be wary. The moment it ceases to do so, you'll regret leaving your tongue unguarded." King Adalberon's words hold a threat that perhaps others would find intimidating, but he is too sane for me to fear.

Before I can make a comment that perhaps later I would regret, King Adalberon continues, apparently having decided to answer my question. "There are a few theories, but no one knows for sure. Our leading scholars seem to believe that the Autumn King did something to anger Faerie, and Faerie cut them off from her like a limb gone bad."

I flinch again and King Adalberon's hand tightens on my waistband. He sounds amused as he asks, "Did that touch a nerve?"

"Why would it?" I say, unable to lie and say it did not.

"Hm-mmm. Perhaps, if you are good, I will bring you to one of the land trows," King Adalberon says, the offer like a blade held over my head.

Be good and he'll let me see a crafter, one who can make me a leg nearly as fine as the one I lost. Don't...and stay like this.

I want to rebel out of pure spite. Will I truly allow another monarch to bend me so easily to their will? Subjugate myself a second time to a being powerful enough to mold me into a stranger?

Do I have a choice?

About the Author

KD Ellis is a queer author of M/M+ romances. They enjoy crafting stories with a bit of angst, a dollop of darkness and always a happy ending! They/them

KD Ellis loves to hear from readers. You can find their contact information, website details and author profile page at https://www.firstforromance.com

ENTWINED PUBLISHING